INFINITE TOMORROW

Lucas Kitchen

LUCAS
KITCHEN
BOOKS

LUCASKITCHEN.COM

ALSO BY LUCAS KITCHEN

Fiction

For The Sake Of The King | Isolation | Missionary To Mars | Cloud Haven | Divine Children | World Builder

Children's Fiction

Good Enough | Adventures Beyond Mudville | Below The Huber Ice | Evan Wants To Go To Heaven

Non-Fiction

Salvation And Discipleship | Eternal Life | Eternal Rewards | Naked Grace | In Pursuit Of Fruit | Eternal Clarity | Things Above | Thomas: Hero Of The Faith

All Available At: Lucaskitchen.com

THE CHOSEN

OSCAR STROLLED BAREFOOT ALONG the cool street. Its surface of polished metal reflected his image. The brilliant sights and wonderful smells of the city surrounded him like a familiar friend, but his mind was elsewhere. The adrenaline was still crackling in his veins from the meeting he had just had. It was an honor to be called to court with the High King, but to be personally assigned a station by him was an unforgettable experience.

"We can't wait to hear about your visit to the mountain, Oscar," a neighbor called as he passed. Oscar waved at the man, a friend he knew well.

"I'd never hear the end of it from my household if they're not the first to hear the tale," Oscar said, smiling. The neighbor laughed as he continued on his way.

He received numerous warm greetings from others who were eager to hear about his adventure. He kindly deflected, knowing that the word would spread soon enough.

Dedicated to my two youngest sons, Leo and Lux.
You guys fill the world with so much laughter!

News traveled fast despite the vastness of the grand city, but it was not proper for a man to brag.

Who would have imagined that a school teacher from First Earth could come so far, he thought. A giggle escaped his lips as he climbed the steps to his house. He didn't let the thought bloom into pride but instead quickly gave thanks to the King for his generous appointment.

The King's words were still ringing in his ears as the automatic door spread wide for his entrance. As soon as he was through the door, he was surrounded. His entourage of attendants and estate managers was eager to hear the news. His household staff waited as Oscar entered the enormous doorway. He was staring at the floor.

"What news from the Court of the High King?" one of his attendants begged. Oscar let the moment swell with anticipation. He looked to each of them as he prepared to relay the news.

"The King has appointed his humble servant as Regent of Newearth," Oscar said. He had no need to hide the joy in his voice. The small audience erupted with a wave of congratulations. Oscar allowed them to enjoy the moment.

Newearth had been a mystery for centuries. The last of the ancient prophecies from First Earth would be fulfilled there, but no one knew how or when that would happen.

Oscar could see the joy of this new revelation in his staff. He was filled with the same feelings of grandeur and was happy to have these closest of friends to share it with.

"The High King's great plan will move forward. We have wondered for many years what will come to pass on Newearth. It seems that we will soon know. All of the Great City will celebrate this day," Oscar said.

His friends hugged and congratulated him further. After a few moments, the chief manager of the house announced, "A celebration is in order, for the master of the house has once again been rewarded for his faithfulness to the King."

All of the staff agreed and began to usher their leader into the greatest of the banquet halls. No expense was spared. The chief sent out invitations to all of Oscar's friends. The entire neighborhood was in the house before an hour had passed. There was music and dancing. More wine than normal was consumed that evening.

After the party was well under way, the attendants began to call for the master of the house to give a speech. After much persuasion, he reluctantly climbed the pedestal at the front of the banquet hall. His words echoed the longing that everyone felt to look into the deep mysteries of the High King.

"My dear friends, you have not come here to honor me, but to honor the King." The crowd exploded with applause. Shouts of praise worshiping the King sounded all over the room. Clapping and impromptu singing rose from the banquet attendees. After a few minutes, the crowd quieted and allowed Oscar to continue.

"I do not know what lies ahead, but I am filled with anticipation for the days to come. Thank you all for your kind celebration." Oscar paused and let the moment grow with a meaningful silence before he continued. "Newearth will finally have human life."

The audience did not breathe a word. They were enthralled at Oscar's speech revelation. They were thirsty for more, although that was almost the entirety of what Oscar knew. He stretched his arms wide and smiled as he increased his volume.

"My home is your home. Stay and celebrate as long as you like. As for me, the High King has called me to Newearth, which is where I am off to now. Thank you, friends."

As soon as he finished speaking, he physically vanished before their eyes. The flash of blue light that marked his space-time jump illuminated the room for a split second. The crowd exploded with applause in praise of the High

King, along with admiration for Oscar's faithfulness. Most of them stayed and celebrated for many hours.

***

THE COOL WIND OF Newearth blew across Oscar's skin. He looked around at the wild place he had landed and said, "Let's get to work."

13 YEARS LATER

THE AIR WAS RICH with a crisp chill. The long shafts of morning light peeked through the trees, where it was already turning the dew into a lingering fog. Oscar loved his trips down to Newearth. They reminded him of his own past. He had spent his first life on a world that was similar. He reminisced as he walked through the garden of mortal boys.

There were no buildings or structures of any kind. The bare simplicity of the green landscape filled him with joy. His twelve students were already up and working at their assignments. Oscar watched each with a fatherly fondness as he walked. He felt a thrill as he thought of the honor it was to train these boys.

"G'morning, Teacher," one of the boys said. Oscar glanced over to see Oseas looking up at him from where he was working on his assignment. Like all of the boys, Oseas was a perfect image of respect and studiousness. The boy quickly went back to working with the plant.

"Hello, Oseas. How is your assignment going?"

"It's going well. I'm finished, but I'm making sure I've made the right choice," Oseas said, but did not look up again. He was cradling a small leafy green plant between his palms and staring at it with intensity. Oscar continued to walk through the midst of the other boys who were in similar postures.

"How about you, Shameless, are you almost finished?" Oscar questioned.

"I am, Sir, but I'm coming up with a backup in case I've chosen poorly." Oscar placed a hand on the boy's shoulder as he responded.

"In this exercise, there is no wrong option. It is up to your creative nature to decide." Shameless looked up at Oscar. A wide smile of satisfaction stretched across his face. Oscar could see that he was enjoying his training.

"In that case, I am finished, Sir."

"Very good."

Oscar continued to walk through the working boys. He thought back to his own former life. Teachers on his home world would have killed to have students like these. He counted eleven clustered near the place of learning. There was one missing. Oscar spun around slowly looking for the twelfth.

"Abriel," he called when he could not find the boy. His eyes roamed the tree line of the garden. From behind a nearby tree trunk, a head popped out. Oscar walked toward him. "Ahh, there you are. How is your assignment going?"

"Fine, I guess," Abriel said.

"Is there something amiss?"

"No, not really." Abriel picked at the bark of the tree and looked up at Oscar. The boy was intelligent and respectful, but Oscar could see something was troubling him. It was strange for anything other than satisfaction to be on the face of any of the boys. Oscar leaned in underneath one of the low-hanging branches.

"Have you chosen a plant yet?" Oscar said.

"Um, well." Abriel looked around quickly. His eyes rested on the tree for a brief second. "I have now."

"Very good," Oscar said with a little chuckle. "You are well on your way to—"

"It's just that—" Abriel began to say, but then stopped himself. "Oh, I'm sorry, Sir, I didn't mean to interrupt."

"It's fine, Abriel. Finish your words."

"It's just that, I'd rather do something else." Abriel looked sheepish, as if he didn't know how to tell anything but the truth, but was a little confused about his own feelings. His candor was refreshing.

"What would you prefer to be doing?" Oscar asked.

"I guess I don't see the purpose of this assignment. I want to do more important things like *you* do."

Oscar let the moment soak in before he said anything. He surveyed him, hoping that there was no seed that could grow into twistedness in the boy. Oscar had seen firsthand what twistedness could do to a world. He spoke slowly, letting Abriel hear the seriousness in his voice.

"The King has said that those who are responsible in small things will be given greater responsibility. Those who have a prominent place in the Great City did not come by it easily," Oscar said. The boy's face lit up at his words.

"I want to go to the Great City. I want to see the shiny streets, and the sea, and the tree-"

"There is a path to that place, and this assignment is along that path." He let an assertive note saturate his tone. Abriel held the gaze of his teacher. There was no defiance in the boy, at least not that Oscar could detect.

"Yes, Sir," Abriel said. He had taken his correction with respect, but the interaction gave Oscar concern. Being the former inhabitant of a bent world, Oscar knew the consequences that misplaced ambition could bring.

"Very good," Oscar said. He smiled and patted Abriel on the shoulder. "It will all make sense in time."

Oscar walked away, still pondering the conversation with his ambitious student. He could feel the creeping concern turning in his stomach. He would not allow it to turn to worry. *It would not be fitting to worry in a place like this,* he thought. He whispered into the cool morning air so softly that none of the boys could hear it.

"My King, I have concern." As soon as the words escaped his lips, he could sense the change. He did not hear the voice as he sometimes did, but he knew the King had responded. He relaxed as the warm peace washed over him. The tension eased, and he released the concern into the open air as he exhaled. "Your plan is good," he breathed.

THE PLANTS

"GATHER, STUDENTS. COME TO the place of learning," Oscar said, loud enough for everyone to hear. Each of the twelve boys moved toward where Oscar was standing. Their enthusiasm was written all over their faces. Oscar noticed the tingle of excitement as he anticipated the lesson he was about to give. His eager pupils soaked up everything he said with almost perfect recollection. When the boys were all seated in the grass before him, Oscar began his talk.

"Greetings, boys. I'm thrilled to be with you today." They all responded in unison with similar comments. Oscar continued. "Your assignment was to choose a plant and name it. We will now share what you have named your plants. Isod, let's begin with you."

Isod was one of the shorter boys, but his zeal overshadowed his lack of height. He stood with a huge smile and spoke so fast that it was hard to understand him. His rapid speech, caused by his excitement, made it sound like his words were slammed together. He only paused when he was forced to breathe.

"Ichosethat purpleshrub bushoverthere. Its-a-really-neat-plant-because-it-has-four—" He paused midstream for a gulp of air. Oscar spoke to him gently.

"Isod, you are excited, I can tell." The boys laughed, as did Isod. He was positively bubbling over. Isod bobbed his head up and down in agreement. Again, the boys giggled. Their levity filled Oscar's heart with warmth. He spoke now with deliberate instruction.

"Even though you are excited, you must speak so that we can understand you. Make your emotions work for you, not against you." Isod nodded, swallowed, and forced himself to slow down.

"I chose that purple shrub bush over there. It's really neat because it has a four-leaf hexagonal stem pattern. The berries that grow on it are really sweet," Isod said, still a little too quickly, but at least it was intelligible.

"Very good, and what have you named it?"

"I've named it," Isod let a pause fill everyone with anticipation. The other boys were riveted. "I've named it Brizzle Berry Bush."

The boys erupted with cheers. They could not contain their excitement. The creative process was new to all of them, and they were hooked. Isod returned to his place with pride.

"That is very good, Isod. Who will go next?" Another boy stood. "Thank you, Eduk. Tell us about your plant." Eduk extended his arm, pointed, and said dramatically.

"That magnificent vine will now be known as The Oasten Fringe." He sat as the boys cheered. Even Oscar put his hands together to show his approval.

Next it was Shameless' turn. He named a wide blade grass Rompstandler. After him, Oseas stood. He named a root vegetable The Longstone Ledgemont. On the boys went. With each new name they grew louder with applause. The ceremony continued with names like, Frizzenbalm, Gorgonfronz, Mangrastein, Abrobasia, Fortenbridge, and the crowd favorite, Sapprosious Contridge Misstaxia.

Each name seemed to fit exactly. It was as if there had been something missing until the names were spoken into existence. The boys tried the new words out as they repeated them to each other. Oscar smiled as he watched the new names roll off their tongues.

All had shared their names except one. The last boy to stand was Abriel. Abriel stepped cautiously to the front of the assembly. He did not have the enthusiasm that the others had displayed. Oscar thought of the conversation they shared beside the tree. Abriel stared at the other boys as he prepared to speak.

"I uh. I guess I picked that tree over there." Abriel pointed. The boys fidgeted before him, seeming not to quite understand his lack of zeal. "I don't know, maybe we could call it-"

He trailed off. He mumbled the name.

"Muzz." The boys stared as if the name was incomplete. There was no applause or celebration. They seemed to sense something was missing. Abriel faltered. He shuffled his feet as he said. "I don't know, maybe I misunderstood the assignment."

"Muzz is a perfectly good name," Oscar assured him. Abriel glanced around nervously.

"I don't know. Maybe it could be something else, like Triff-" he watched the boys for feedback, and gathered that they wanted more. "Or like Triffle." Their eyes were still begging. "Uh, it makes sticks...stick... Triffle Stick... Triffle Stick Tree. I guess." Some of the boys seemed moderately satisfied now.

"Well, which is it? Muzz, or Trifflestick Tree?" Shameless questioned.

Oscar watched Abriel begin to come unraveled. He wasn't dealing well with the group pressure. Abriel seemed to harden as he responded to Shameless.

"I changed my mind," Abriel said sternly. Frustration stretched tight across his face. He looked directly at Shameless as he added, "That tree has no name. It will be the unnamed tree."

The boys muttered to each other as Abriel sat down in a huff. It disappointed Oscar to see the tension between his students. He moved back to the front of the group and regained their attention.

"Thank you, Students. You have named your first plant. This will not be the last-"

"Wait, Abreil didn't name his tree," Shameless said. Some of the other boys spoke up as well.

"On the contrary, Shameless. He did name his tree." Oscar's words hushed the class. The boys' faces twisted in confusion. "He named it The Unnamed Tree. Is that not a name?"

The seeming contradiction danced around the group. Their confusion swelled large for a few seconds until it burst like a bubble. Isod was the first to get it. He made a sound of understanding and then laughed. Others seemed to get it then, and laughter began to fill the air. Even Abriel's hard shell cracked as he joined in the levity.

"He meant to give it no name, but by doing so, he gave it a name. It makes my head hurt," Shameless said. He dropped back into another round of giggling. "What do you call that?"

"That is a paradox," Oscar said. He loved their joy in the simplest of discoveries. As the laughter began to die down, another spoke up.

"We like paradoxes, will you teach us another?" Oseas said. Oscar thought for a second before he shared.

"I will tell you one from the world I come from." He let the anticipation build. "Is the answer to this question no?"

They all sat completely silent for a few seconds. After a long pause, Eduk put both hands to his head and made a howling sound as if the question was scrambling his brain. Oscar laughed as did everyone else. He let them enjoy the paradox for another minute before he gathered their attention again.

"Students, you see the joy of learning. You have learned the meaning of a paradox. I look forward to hearing what paradoxes you come up with. However, that is not the subject of today's lesson."

The boys concentrated their attention on Oscar as he prepared to teach them. They were eager to find out whatever Oscar had to share.

A HARD LESSON

"TODAY WE WILL BEGIN to learn a very important skill, but first I will tell you about the world I came from." The boys shifted eagerly as they waited for the tasty treat Oscar was about to provide.

"In the first Earth, there was a time when plants, animals, and men were in harmony. The plants grew the way they were told. The animals played their role as they should. However, the men became bent to the point of breaking. They rebelled against the King's natural order, and became deaf and dumb."

The boys seemed uneasy at the story. It was the first they had heard of the former Earth, and they were not used to stories with such elements. Oscar could see their discomfort.

"A great many things became twisted. The first but not the greatest loss was the natural order. People could no longer communicate with the plants or beasts. We lost our ability to cultivate harmoniously. We were left with only brute force to use on the plants and animals to get them to do what we wanted and needed. We broke our world with our rebellion. If it were not for the King, we would have destroyed it."

The boys gasped. They could not imagine such a place. Oscar knelt down and spoke more gently to them. He drove the story home with a gestured depiction.

"We would rip plants from the ground and place them in new settings. Many plants died at our hands." The boys recoiled. The look of disbelief washed over them all. Oscar was afraid he might leave them with emotional scars, so he relented. "And these actions were the least bent of my world's. The greater of my world's wrongs are not to be named here, for they may very well turn your hearts to stone."

Some of the students clutched at their chests as if they would protect their hearts. Oscar softened at their innocence. He was sad that even the knowledge of such things should be in these twelve children.

"However, the old things have passed away, and the new has come. When the first Earth was nearly destroyed, the King came to set the natural order right again. He came to show the world how to repair what we had broken."

Oscar stood from his squatting position and gestured for the boys to follow. They all stood and surrounded Oscar as he walked toward the edge of the garden. The boys were bouncing with anticipation. Oscar stopped near the hedge that marked the end of the garden and pointed out beyond.

"Out there are the wilds." He turned and pointed inward toward the garden. It was a stark contrast. "In here is the garden." The boy's eyes flitted from one to the other. Oscar could tell their imaginations were running wild.

"Why is it different out there?" Abriel asked. Oscar was glad to see him engaged. He turned toward the boy to answer his question.

"It is like that out there because the wilds have no teacher. Not yet, that is."

The boys thought about this in silence as they stared out at the twisted patches of vines and branches. Oscar wondered what they were thinking. The forest that stretched beyond the edge of the haven they were in was dark and brooding.

Oscar could sense their wonder as twelve sets of eyes looked out beyond the edge of their known world. He imagined what these boys, these men-to-be, would someday do with this green, overgrown world.

"What are you, Abriel?" Oscar asked. The question obviously took him by surprise. He allowed the student a minute to consider.

"A boy."

"Yes, but what else?"

"A student," he said. This time, it sounded more like a question. Oscar reached out for his shoulder and gave him a pat.

"That's right, but from now on, you will be both a student and a teacher. All of you will. Ahh, there is another paradox for you." The boys did not giggle this time. It felt much more serious than it had before.

"How can we be both students and teachers?" Shameless asked. Oscar turned and began to walk back toward the center of the garden. He spoke to them as they followed along.

"Just as you need a teacher, so do the plants. In time, even the beasts will be your students. You have their language in you, but it is a language you have not yet used. You must work at it. Someday, you will even tame the wilds."

Oscar glanced around as they walked back to the place of learning. He could see that they were all contemplating the things he had said.

"So why does the garden look the way it does?" Oseas asked.

"Because the plants in the garden had a teacher," Oscar said as he knelt down and reached out for the patch of vines that Eduk had named. He touched them near the root and spoke softly. "Oasten Fringe, from now on, you are to grow fruit that is good for eating."

They watched with wide eyed wonder as Oscar stood. They waited as if it were going to happen before their eyes. Oscar watched them for a moment before he let out a hearty laugh. His laugh confused the boys. Their attention shifted to him.

"You have to be patient with plants, they move much slower than you do. Instructions may take days or even weeks to fulfill. In time, you will learn to work with all kinds of plants."

"Can I try?" one of the boys asked.

"That is your assignment. From now until I return, you are to try what I have shown you. It will take patience and persistence. Don't expect results right away. It is not with words that the plants change, but with the deeper intention that the words represent. The biggest plants will move the slowest, so extra patience will be required with them."

"Too bad you chose the Unnamed Tree, Abriel. It's huge," one of the boys said. Abriel didn't respond.

IN THE GARDEN

ABRIEL WOKE. THAT WITHIN itself was nothing strange. However, something was different. Abriel was vaguely aware of an odd sensation. It was something he had never experienced before. From his earliest memories, he had always woken to the world with joy and wonder. This morning, those sensations were there, but they were not the only ones.

He sat up in the grass where he had lain for the night. The other boys were already up. Oseas was climbing in a tree nearby. Abriel could hear the jubilant laughter of eleven others. As he looked around the garden, he tried to identify the feelings that were below his surface.

It was as if the joy that he was feeling was less than it could be. Or was it less than it *should* be? Abriel thought of his teacher's story of the former world. The broken race of men who became twisted. A sneaking concern grew in his stomach.

He placed his hands in the dewy grass and stood. Eduk bolted by with a giggle. Trailing behind him was a little four-legged creature. Abriel had seen one before, but like most things in the garden, it did not yet have a name. Eduk ducked behind a tree to evade the little animal. The spectacle of their playful game was a temporary distraction. Eduk popped his head out from behind the tree and spoke to no one in particular.

"This little animal will now be called a Squash Waddle," Eduk said. The other boys who were nearby cheered loudly at the new name. Eduk bolted from behind the tree, allowing the little creature to nearly touch him. "Catch me if you can, Squash Waddle."

The boys who watched laughed. Abriel could hear his garden brothers beginning to name other creatures that were around. Oseas called out from the high tree branch he was on. Letting everyone know that the name of the six-legged branch bug was "Logtrotter." The other boys howled with excitement.

Abriel was not as interested as he normally would have been. Instead, he thought breakfast might be a more satisfying activity. He walked to a nearby bush, known among the boys for its chunky nuts. He pulled a handful and cracked them between his palms. As he threw the shelled meat into his mouth, he surveyed the garden.

It is a splendid place, so why do I feel like this? He thought. He let his eyes range over the hedges that hemmed in his world. He stared out past the edge at the wilds. He found himself wondering how far they went. He let his eyes drop to the garden floor. The dew was beginning to burn off in the morning sun.

That's when he saw it. He dropped his handful of nuts as he stared. Could it be? Was his mind playing tricks? Hanging from the Oasten Fringe vine was something. It was something he'd never noticed before. Abriel stepped closer to investigate. He knelt down and reached out for it.

The previous afternoon, Oscar had spoken to this very vine. He had given it instructions to grow fruit that is good for eating. As Abriel's fingers grazed the buds that were now growing, he marveled at the magic of it.

"The King's world is good," he whispered to himself, as he had heard Oscar say a number of times.

He squeezed the newly forming fruit between his thumb and index. Pulling the grape-like sprout from the vine, he placed it on his tongue. He could not help but to coo with excitement. His mood began to climb as the sweet juice filled his mouth.

"Hey, what's that?" Shameless said from over Abriel's shoulder. "Oh wow! Hey everybody, Abriel has found a new fruit on the Oasten Fringe."

As if their former joy was only a preamble, the boys dropped whatever they were doing and came over to see. One by one, they plucked the fruit from the Oasten Fringe and tasted. The enjoyment was unanimous.

"It's incredible," Shameless said.

"It grew quick," Isod added. After the vine was picked completely clean, the boys stood and stared for a short moment. Apparently, the same thought hit them all at about the same time.

"I'm going to go work on my assignment," Oseas said with exuberance. One by one, the rest of the boys agreed. Seeing the results of Oscar's lesson so soon inspired them to try their hand at cultivation. The rest of them fanned out and began speaking to the plants they had previously named.

The air was electric. Even Abriel could sense the hope in all of it. To think that he would be not only a namer of his world, but a shaper as well, was almost more than he could conceive. It wasn't long before Abriel had forgotten the slight off shade of his morning's mood.

DISCOURAGED

"UNNAMED TREE, YOU ARE to grow branches low to the ground so that I can climb up easily," Abriel said. He was almost certain the tree was not hearing him. Oscar had told them that they must be patient. Something as large as a tree would take time to respond to the instructions, but Abriel was sure he needed more training to do his assignment correctly.

He repeated his words, thinking that maybe by repetition something would occur. Once he had spoken to the tree's enormous trunk a number of times without any noticeable success, he stepped back and stared.

Abriel could hear the other boys murmuring softly to their pupil plants in the distance. He wondered if anyone else was having as little success as he was. His puzzlement grew into distraction as he looked around at the others. He caught sight of Isod about twenty paces away. He focused his attention on hearing what Isod was saying.

"Brizzle Berry, I want you to begin to grow taller," Isod said as he watched the shrubby bush intently. The excitement that was written on his face was obvious even from a distance. Isod's eyes began to grow. Abriel held his breath as Isod shouted out, "It's working. It's growing new sprigs."

Some of the other boys rushed over to see Isod's revelation. Abriel did not want a closer look. It would only serve as a reminder that he did not know what he was doing. Abriel tuned out the noise that Isod's success caused among the others. He focused back on the Unnamed Tree.

He let his eyes follow the tree's leafy lines upward. It seemed like it was as tall as the sky itself. His mind wandered out past the end of the branches of the unnamed giant. He stared into the vibrant blue of the sky that stretched on to the edge of forever.

As he watched the brilliant glowing light peeking through the tree, he breathed in the garden smells. The light warmed his face where it blazed through the breaks in the canopy. His eyes followed the shining point in the sky as it rose up through the open space above.

It was almost too bright to look at, but he couldn't help himself. He stared as it drifted lazily through the distant sky. The Great City, as Oscar had called it, cast warmth and light on all of Newearth below. Abriel was filled with questions. *What were they doing up there?* He thought. Oscar's description of the Great City danced through Abriel's mind as he watched it slowly cross the sky.

Abriel imagined himself there. He imagined walking on the streets of polished metal. He envisioned himself owning a mansion. He longed to sip water from the crystal clear sea, whatever that was. He didn't understand any of it, but he wanted to go so badly that it almost hurt.

Abriel was pulled from his daydream when he felt a hand lightly on his shoulder. He turned to find Oscar, his teacher, looking down at him.

"Abriel, I've been calling your name," Oscar said.

"I'm sorry. I didn't see you arrive."

"Is something wrong?" Oscar asked. Abriel crinkled his nose up as he had a habit of doing when he didn't understand something. He thought about the question for a long moment before he responded.

"Wrong?" Abriel repeated. He had heard the word only once before. Oscar had used it in his lesson the previous day. "What does the word 'wrong' mean?" he asked.

"Oh, right. I forget. I assume too much. It's a word from the former world." Oscar paused. "Wrong means-" Oscar started, but then stopped again. Abriel had never seen him without adequate words. It was strange to watch him search for the right way to describe what he meant. He finally started again, but with a question this time.

"What is your favorite fruit in the garden?"

"The new Oasten Fringe grape," Abriel replied.

"Does it taste like a grape should taste?"

"It does," Abriel said.

"Have you ever tasted the things in the garden that are not for eating? For instance, the dirt, or the bark of a tree?"

"Yes, we all have tasted them, but only once."

"Very good. Now imagine that you pulled a grape from the Oasten Fringe branch and tasted it, but it tasted as it should not. Imagine that it tasted like the dirt that you have tried once," Oscar said. Abriel imagined it for a moment before he responded.

"That would be an unexpected discovery," Abriel said.

"Yes, it would. Now, imagine that you had been told that all grapes are sweet, but you had found this grape to be otherwise. What would that mean?"

"It would mean that I do not understand the word sweet, or that the statement is incorrect, or that it is not a grape," Abriel said.

"Yes. Very Good. However, imagine that you are certain that it is a grape, you are certain of the meaning of sweet, and you are certain that the statement is true."

Abriel contorted his face into a wrinkle as the thought sent rivers of confusion across his mind. He could not conceive of a logical explanation for all three to be true. He wanted to understand, but he could not grasp the meaning. Suddenly, something clicked into place.

"It is a paradox," Abriel said, although it felt only like an escape, not an explanation. Oscar smiled.

"Yes, it is. When things are not how they should be, that is the meaning of the word wrong."

Abriel looked out beyond the edge of the garden as he thought about Oscar's words. He sensed that they were not actually talking about the taste of grapes.

"So are we using the grape to talk about something that is not a grape?"

"Very good," Oscar congratulated with a laugh. "It's called a parable. The King used them in the former world to teach us of the things of the future world."

"I think I see a kind of meaning in it," Abriel said.

"Tell me what you see."

"When you spoke of the grape, tasting a way it should not taste, it made me think of my feelings." Oscar knelt down to be eye level with Abriel. He waited for him to continue. "When I woke this morning, I may have felt some wrongness."

Abriel turned to look up at the Great City floating through the sky. The light made him squint. He wanted to get answers.

"Can you describe it?" Oscar asked. Now Abriel searched for the words. He found that he did not have any that fit what he wanted to say. He took a breath as if he would speak, but nothing came out. He tried to relax his mind and take a new approach. Suddenly, an image sprang to his mind.

"It's as if there is a fruit on a branch that is too high to reach. I think it may be too high because I am not meant to reach it, but I want it nonetheless." Abriel felt proud of his use of a parable. He hoped he had used it correctly.

Oscar pondered this for a long moment before he spoke. His tone was smooth and slow. He portrayed no hint that there was wrongness in the feeling.

"And what is it that you want?" Oscar asked.

"I want to go to the Great City. Is this a wrongness to want this?" Abriel asked with concern in his eyes.

"The wanting of a thing is not a wrongness in itself. It is the result of the wanting where wrongness can occur."

"So do you mean that I have not become twisted, as the ones of your world became twisted?" Abriel's eyes were wide with anticipation. Oscar reached his hand out and placed it on Abriel's shoulder as he had a habit of doing.

He spoke with a warmth that made Abriel feel deeply cared for.

"You are not twisted, my student. The rending of a world is not a thing that can pass unnoticed." Oscar removed his hand from his shoulder and stood. "To want is what drives us to discovery. It is our thirst that makes us strong. It is our desire that gives us a deeper life."

Abriel smiled. His teacher always seemed to have the perfect words. He was filled with hope and joy again. After a moment, a wondering question shot across Abriel's mind.

"Teacher, do you or any of the other Elvangaleen ever have a wrongness?" Abriel asked. Oscar began walking and gestured Abriel to follow along. They walked toward the Unnamed Tree as Oscar answered.

"We Elvangaleen, who live in the Great City are not able to have a wrongness. The ones of us from the former Earth once were able, but we have been changed by the King. We are, however, able to feel a lesser joy."

"What is a lesser joy?" Abriel asked. Oscar stopped next to the tree and placed his hand on the trunk.

"Do you know why I was chosen to be your teacher?"

"No," Abriel said.

"I was chosen based on my faithfulness in the previous world. I could have done more to show my loyalty to the

King. I live knowing that had I been more faithful then, I would have had more joy now. The reward in this Kingdom is closeness to the King. Had I been more faithful in my previous life, I would have been closer to him now. That is what a lesser joy means."

Oscar turned toward the trunk of the tree and ran his fingers down the bark. He looked closely as if he were searching for something. He knelt as his hands slid toward the dirt. He stopped and looked up at Abriel when he found what he was searching for.

"I see you have been working on your assignment," Oscar said. Abriel raised his eyebrows in excitement. He had not noticed any change. He moved quickly to see what his teacher was seeing. Oscar added, "Place your fingers here on the trunk. You can feel the beginning of a branch for climbing."

Abriel grazed the bark as Oscar stepped back. He had assumed that he had done his assignment incorrectly. He was elated to discover anything to the contrary. As he pressed into the bark he could feel a small bulge in the skin of the tree. Oscar watched him as he filled with the joy of discovery.

"I thought the tree did not hear me."

"The tree heard, but everything grows at a different speed," Oscar said.

Abriel smiled as he asked, "Are you teaching me by a parable now?"

"I sure am," Oscar responded.

WILD FRIENDS

"GATHER, STUDENTS. EVERYONE TO the place of learning," Oscar said, loud enough for everyone to hear. Within seconds, the twelve boys were assembled. Abriel was the last to arrive. He had been admiring the progress of The Unnamed Tree. When the boys were all seated in the grass in front of Oscar, he began to speak.

"I've looked quickly at each of your assignments. I'm very proud of you. They are all very good."

The boys were overjoyed with the affirmation. They could barely contain themselves. To Abriel, the excitement was infectious.

"When will we be able to tame the wilds?" Shameless asked. Oscar smiled as he surveyed the boys' faces. The question belonged not only to Shameless but to all the boys.

"Very good," Oscar said. "Your enthusiasm is admirable. However, to tame the wilds, you will need help."

"Are there other boys like us in the wilds?" Oseas asked.

"There are no other boys in Newearth. However, someday there will be," Oscar said. Rather than move on, he waited for their next question. Abriel was filled with wonder, but Isod beat him to the question.

"How will there be more boys in the world someday if there are none now?" Isod asked.

"Honestly, Students, I do not know," Oscar said. The boys gasped. They had never heard those words come from the mouth of their teacher. Abriel had assumed that Oscar's knowledge was endless. To reach the end of his knowledge was a strange feeling. "But, I do know that the King's plan is good."

"Who will help us tame the wilds if there are no other boys?" Abriel asked. It was not the thing that Abriel wanted to know the most, but it was the next obvious question. Instead of answering directly, Oscar turned away from the boys and shouted toward the edge of the garden.

"Mordecai. Mordecai. Mordecai!"

The boys stood where they were to see what Oscar was calling out to. They stared off past the edge of the garden, waiting for something to happen. When nothing did, Oscar called out one more time.

A deep bellowing blast came from the darkness of the vines and trees beyond the hedge. It sounded like the call of a mighty beast. Through his feet, Abriel could feel the rumbling of the ground, as if massive trees were falling in the distance. Abriel and his companions watched as something large emerged from the woods.

"There you are, you silly thing," Oscar called to it.

It was the most enormous beast Abriel, or any of the boys had ever seen. From the tip of its head to the ground was at least as tall as the unnamed tree. Abriel held his breath in wonder. The creature bellowed again. He could feel the rumble of its voice vibrating his chest.

The giant creature plodded powerfully toward the place of learning. It stopped and stood next to where Oscar was standing. It made Oscar look like an ant next to its gigantic size. Oscar reached up his hand toward the huge animal. The creature craned his long neck low and allowed Oscar to climb on top. Oscar sat on the animal's head as it raised back up to its full height. He addressed them now with a loud voice.

"This is Mordecai. In my world, his kind were called Brachiosaurus. Mordecai helped me build this garden." Oscar had to shout to be heard from up high on the animal's head. Abriel let his eyes follow the lines of the huge creature.

Mordecai's head was massive, but small compared to his body. His neck looked like the trunk of a tree and seemed to stretch into the sky. Even his tail was bigger than any single creature Abriel had ever seen. He looked back up at Oscar, who was still perched on Mordecai's head.

"A friend like Mordecai is handy when you need a little help, or when you need a big help. The plants respond to cultivation, but dirt and rocks don't. You can thank Mordecai for the level ground that you now stand on."

Oscar patted Mordecai on the side of the head. He responded by lowering his neck slowly back toward the ground. When his head was in the grass, Oscar climbed off and patted him again.

"Good boy," Oscar said as he gave the huge beast a slap on the side of the neck. The Brachiosaurus let out a joyful bellow. Oscar laughed as if there was something to be understood in the unintelligible noise. Oscar turned back to the students. The boys' eyes stayed on Mordecai as Oscar spoke.

"Abriel, you asked who would help you tame the wilds. You now have your answer," Oscar said.

"Can we talk to them?" Isod asked.

"In a manner, you can. However, your speech is too complicated for most beasts. You have the mind to learn their language, all but a few do not have the mind to learn yours."

"Why haven't we seen anything like Mordecai before?" Oseas asked.

"You will find that the animals of Newearth are drawn to you. Until now, my fellow Elvangaleen have kept all but small beasts out of the garden. The beasts of the surrounding wilds will now be allowed to come into the garden. When you are ready, and you have gained proper partners, you will begin to tame the wilds together."

"Why was the Brachiosaurus made so powerful, and we are so weak?" Abriel asked.

"The King designed each of us with certain strengths to do certain tasks. With certain strengths come deliberate limitations. The King has given you the most powerful mind of all the creatures, but has left your body small so that partnerships with creatures like Mordecai can prove most rewarding."

Abriel noticed movement near the edge of the garden. He focused his eyes, trying to see the cause. Through the hedge of the garden came crawling a four legged creature that Abriel had never seen. It was not the only one. A few paces away another came bouncing through over the line of bushy plants. Before long there were creatures of all kinds approaching. They waddled, crawled, slithered, and flew.

A MISSION WAITS

WITHIN A MATTER OF a few minutes the surrounding gardened area was full of creatures of all shapes, colors and sizes. The boys marveled at the assortment of life, the likes of which they had never dreamed. Abriel looked to Oscar expecting some further explanation.

"Your assignment until I return is to name these animals and begin to learn their language," Oscar said. He then smiled and added, "Have fun."

The other boys could not be contained. As soon as Oscar finished speaking they were off. They spread out and began to play with all of the creatures. It was a peaceful chaos. As Oscar had said the animals were drawn to the boys. Likewise the boys seemed to be drawn to the creatures. However, Abriel had his mind on something else. Before Oscar could leave Abriel called out to him.

"Teacher?" he said.

"Yes."

"I have a question, but I do not want to act ungrateful for what we have learned," Abriel said. He had to speak loudly to be heard over the noise that was growing around them. Oscar stepped close to hear.

"You may ask."

"I see creatures that can fly. I see creatures of many sizes. Is there a flying creature that can take me to the Great City?" Abriel said. He wondered if he should not have asked. He had learned that some questions are better than others, and this might have been a question that is less good. Oscar thought for a few seconds before he responded.

"Even with all of this, you still are thinking of the Great City?"

"Yes. Is that a wrongness?" Abriel asked.

"It is not a wrongness." Oscar turned and began to walk. He gestured for Abriel to join him. "Come, let us talk away from the noise."

They walked toward the edge. Creatures were still crawling through the hedges to join the activity at the heart of the garden. Oscar stopped and turned toward his student. It was quieter, so Abriel found it easier to focus.

"Abriel, as you know, you are the firstborn in Newearth. This means that you are likely to possess many of the firsts."

The first part, Abriel knew; the second part, he did not. His mind soared like the birds he had just seen. He imagined what it might mean to possess firsts.

"Among many other things, you will be the first to become a man."

"What is a man?" Abriel said. The idea of becoming anything but what he already was felt strange. He tried the word on within his mind.

"Just like a sprig is a tree, but not a fully formed tree, a boy is a man, but not a fully grown man," Oscar explained. Abriel turned the idea over in his mind. He compared himself to a sprig. He easily saw the logic in it, but could not grasp what being a man meant.

"Is the reason I desire things I do not possess because I'm becoming a man?" Abriel asked.

"I believe it is, Abriel. A man seeks adventure. A man seeks to know what he does not already know, even if it means that he must venture far to learn. You have asked me if it is a wrongness to desire. It is not a wrongness, but it is a newness. It is the kind of newness that comes with becoming a man."

Abriel turned to look out into the wilds. He ran his hand along the leafy stalks of the hedges that divided his world from the outside. He wondered what would be done with him. Oscar spoke slowly as if what he had to say was more important than all the rest.

"This garden is for boys. It is not the home of men," Oscar said. Abriel's breath caught in his throat. His eyes darted up to Oscar's solemn face. Oscar stared back at him with solidarity. He could hardly believe what he had just heard.

"Am I to leave?" Abriel asked. Oscar only nodded. "Am I to leave now?"

"You are not yet a man, but the time is soon."

"Am I to go to the Great City?" Abriel asked with excitement. His eyes grew wide with anticipation. He imagined the stories Oscar had told of the Great City.

"The Great City is not the home of mortal men. Your home is here on Newearth."

Abriel deflated slightly. He did not want to disappoint his teacher, but he was filled with confusion. There was a kind of hope buried deep below the surface, but what he wanted he could not have. Oscar took a deep breath and looked up at the Great City. The shadows were getting long as it neared the horizon.

"What you want is not always what you need. It is important to use the desire for what you want, to find the thing you truly need," Oscar said.

Abriel tried his best to understand what his teacher was telling him. He had not yet completely grasped the meaning of paradoxes and sensed that this one was a difficult one. Abriel waited for more explanation, but instead, Oscar knelt down and spoke intensely.

"The time for your mission has come," Oscar said.

"What does that mean?"

"It means I have a task for you that will take you away from the garden."

"What is it?" Abriel asked. Oscar stood again and watched the other boys playing with the new creatures in the garden.

"Many days' journey from here is a great mountain. It's a mountain so great that even Mordecai could not move it with a hundred of his own kind. On the far side of that mountain grows a single flower. It is the only of its kind. You must go and name that flower, and help it to grow."

Abriel stared at him in confusion. He could not figure out why the task was so disconnected from the conversation they were having. He rolled it over in his mind, trying to see the meaning, but he couldn't make sense of it.

"I do not understand," Abriel said.

"To understand is not the task."

"I thought that this task would be a kind of answer to the questions that we were discussing," Abriel said. "It seems that the task has nothing to do with any of it. I have named plants here and helped them to grow. Why is there a need for me to go such a great distance to see a single flower?"

"Are you declining the task?"

"May I have a different task?" Abriel requested sheepishly.

"This is the one for you."

Abriel fidgeted, something that he had rarely ever done. The feelings that were racing through him were strange. There was a mixture of excitement at the prospect of adventure but a sense that something would be lost if he left the garden. Oscar smiled as he spoke.

"I can see that you are full of confusion. I will offer something that will help you decide. If you take and complete the task, I will take you to the Great City."

Abriel nearly jumped out of his skin. He could barely believe what he had just heard. A boyish grin stretched across his face as he watched the expression of his teacher.

"I will accept the task," Abriel nearly shouted. His blood pumped like a river, and his breaths became deep and rich. He cared nothing for the task, but he would do it in order to receive a visit to the Great City.

"You will need a helper and guide," his teacher said. "I will go and prepare one suited for the task."

Abriel thought of the possibilities. He imagined a giant flying creature that could take him to the peak. Maybe instead, Oscar would prepare one like Mordecai, who could push all of the wild vines and trees that stood in his way. Even better would be a swift-footed creature that could make the journey in hours instead of days. All Abriel knew was that he wanted to get the task over with so he could finally see the Great City.

NO RETURN

ABRIEL COULD NOT SLEEP that night. It never got completely dark on Newearth, so he stared up at the stars from where he lay on his back in the grass. The glow of the Great City lingered low on the horizon as it made its oblong orbit.

Abriel sighed aloud as he watched the sky. He wondered what was waiting for him beyond the edge of the garden. He was brimming with exotic excitement as he imagined his visit to the Great City.

Oscar had told him about the gold that were made of streets, or something like that. Abriel didn't know what that meant but he knew that it would be a spectacle to behold. He sat up in the grass where he had been trying to sleep for three or four hours. Looking around he saw the other boys snoozing comfortably.

Oseas was lying with drooped arms and legs over a tree branch. A cool night breeze played softly with the leaves.

Isod and Shameless lay nearby in the grass. The other boys had taken up various sleeping locations around the peaceful garden. Abriel felt a strange mix of feelings as he imagined leaving. How was it possible to feel so much at one time? Part of him wanted to stay, but the larger part of him was ready for the journey.

He stood and walked toward the hedge that rimmed his gardened world. He lingered there as he stared out into the wilds. The low starlight rimmed the trees and vines in the thicket beyond. This blooming hamlet had been his entire world, but he could feel the distant draw of adventure wooing him outward.

Oscar had intended Abriel to wait until he returned with his guide. Abriel was having a hard time keeping his anticipation from ruling his mind. He found himself wondering what would happen if he went ahead and set out on his journey.

"Teacher did not actually say I *had* to wait," Abriel whispered to himself as if he wasn't convinced. It was technically true. Even though there was no direct instruction, it felt strange to even consider violating Oscar's intentions. Abriel glanced back at the other boys, where they slept. He had no idea what they would do if they woke and found one of their garden brothers missing. Abriel could see himself leaving. His heart pounded as he considered it.

"Teacher is an Elvangaleen. He can appear anywhere he wants. I could begin my journey, and he could come to me on my way," Abriel said, trying to reassure himself that it was reasonable. His eyes bulged and his breath caught in his throat as he moved toward the hedge.

The bushes that lined the boundary of the garden were about waist high. Abriel ran his hand tentatively along the top of the hedge as he considered what he was about to do. He courted the idea as he allowed it to grow intimate with his mind. He could see a kind of bravery in it.

Maybe Teacher will even commend me for my courage, he thought. He felt something happen in his mind. It was as if something clicked into place. It was decided. *This is probably what Teacher wanted me to do,* Abriel thought.

He shoved his hands into the hedge and pushed them apart in order to make a place to pass through. The bush separated easily as he pressed his body between. He had to shimmy a little to squeeze through. Without much effort, he was beyond the hedge and out of the garden. He had expected to feel something, but apparently nothing had changed.

He took one step but then froze. *What am I doing,* He thought. *This was not what Teacher wanted.* He looked back into the garden. He suddenly felt as if he'd been confused. He could see it clearly now. Oscar had intended him to wait. Looking into the garden made him feel a kind of lesser joy. He wished that he had taken no action.

He turned fully toward the garden and moved quickly. He had to go back. He knew that he must wait for the guide that Oscar would bring. He knew he had acted brashly. He wanted to undo his action. He would go back to sleep and pretend this never happened. He took another step toward the hedge that was still split. He reached out for it to make his path back in.

Suddenly, a great flash of light erupted in front of his face. He felt a concussion strike him in the chest. It did not hurt as much as it startled him. Before he knew what was happening, he felt air rushing by. He flew back with the impact and landed roughly on the ground. He flopped in a heap near a circle of wild trees.

It took him a second to recover from the scare. He stood and dusted himself off. The place he had landed was about ten paces back from the hedge. There were wild vines and branches all around him. Abriel strained his eyes to see what could have caused the impact.

When he saw nothing in the air or on the ground nearby, he moved toward the hedge more cautiously this time. He reached out with his hand, hoping he could save himself from being struck a second time. As he approached the hedge once more, he noticed something peculiar.

With each step, a shimmering light began to glow brighter, hovering over the path he had made through the bushes. The closer he got, the brighter it became. When he was only a few paces away from his entrance back into the garden, the light was bright enough for him to make out a shape. Abriel stopped and watched the light as it began to illuminate the hedge and the wild ground around.

Abriel stepped back instinctively. His hand found its way to his chest where he had been struck. As the lighted shape became more brilliant Abriel could see that it made the outlined form of a person. He had to squint when the light became almost too bright to bear. Abriel placed his hands in front of his eyes to shield himself.

Through the cracks between his fingers, Abriel tried to see the shining man. Light poured from him like the Great City itself. Abriel had never seen anything like it. A thunderous sound poured from the illuminated figure. Abriel realized that it was a voice, but it was impossibly powerful.

"There is but one leaving for each man-child.
He shall never return from the far wild.
Until all path and forest be cultivated,
And flower and boy be not separated."

It was as if the voice echoed off the distant mountains, the wild trees, and rumbled the deepest part of Abriel's soul. He knew that the proclamation was intended for him. He wasn't sure of its complete meaning but it was clear that Abriel would not be able to enter the garden again.

He was surprised to find that he was involuntarily shaking. He did not understand his quivering but could sense that it had something to do with the Shining Man's radiance and his own weakness.

Abriel continued to stare where the brilliant Elvangaleen had been. As his eyes adjusted back to the darkness, he could now see over the hedge. The starlit scene that stared back showed him what he had lost. Eleven sets of eyes watched from the other side of the hedge. The other boys regarded him for a long moment with confusion. The shimmering light of the Elvangaleen was totally gone. In its place stood only regret.

The voice of the Elvangaleen had apparently woken the other boys. They all looked to Abriel as if they could not understand what was happening. Isod was the first to move. He reached for the hedge as if he too were going to crawl through.

"No!" Abriel cried. His fervor startled Isod and the others. "Do not come through the hedge. You cannot return to the garden once you've left."

"Why then have you gone through the hedge?" Shameless asked. Bewilderment was painted across his face.

"I should not have done it."

"Why then did you do a thing you should not have done?" Oseas asked. His innocent tone stabbed at Abriel. The look in his and the other boys' eyes spoke deeper and colder than their words ever could.

"I am not sure, but I think I may have become bent. I may have done a wrongness," Abriel said with more emotion than he had ever had cause to use. "Promise me you will not follow me."

"Are we not meant to live as twelve? How will we now live as eleven? It has never been done in the history of Newearth," Eduk said.

"My brothers, I am sorry."

With that, Abriel turned and ran into the deep, dark woods. The wilds surrounded him as the sound of his brothers' voices died away at his back. His lungs gushed sweet night air as his blood streamed like rivers through his legs. He felt, for the first time in his life, that he was alone.

A VOICE

THE WILDS WERE TERRIBLY wild. It was not easy moving through the vines and branches that hung way too low. Abriel crept through the woods as the day passed. Because of his lack of instruction, the movement could not even be called progress.

From the canopy to the forest floor, the wilds were full of all kinds of animal life. Birds zipped by with stunning grace and beauty. Small creatures scampered near his feet and up trees as he passed. He had even seen a few larger animals as he worked his way through the underbrush.

He could not imagine being tasked with cultivating all of the wild places. It made him want to be in the Great City even more. He glanced toward the sky that was obscured by the tops of the powerful trees. He wished he could get a look at the massive floating city. He wondered if he would ever see it. He pressed the thought out of his mind as he pushed back a handful of vines.

"Abriel, why have you left the garden?" a voice said.

"Teacher?" Abriel said. An unstoppable joy washed over him as he turned and looked about to see Oscar. He spun around once, then twice, but could not find him. "Where are you, Teacher?"

"I am not permitted to come to you except in the garden until your task is complete."

"I hear your voice, are you not close by?" Abriel asked.

"My voice is nearby, but my body is not." He paused. He spoke softly. "Why have you left the garden?"

Abriel wanted to give an answer, but the truth confused him. He was not sure why he had left. He had been trying to understand all day, but the words did not express what he felt. He tried anyway.

"I don't know. I thought I should," Abriel said. He closed his eyes as he prepared to ask the question whose answer he was not sure he was ready to receive. "Have I done a wrongness? Have I become twisted?"

A long pause sat between Abriel and the voice of his Teacher. The tension filled him with anticipation. He wanted to repeat the question louder. Abriel opened his eyes and exhaled as he whispered.

"Teacher?"

"I am sorry for the delay, I had to look upon you to know the answer to your question. To look from such a great distance takes concentration. However, I can see that you have not done a wrongness. You have not become twisted, my student."

Abriel could have leaped for joy. It was as if a weight was lifted from his shoulders. He took a deep breath as he soaked in the moment. He had not realized that his concern had been sitting so heavy on his mind all morning and early afternoon.

"Why then, did the Elvangaleen keep me from going back into the garden?" Abriel asked.

"It is the way of things. Once a boy leaves, he is not to return to the garden of his youth. This was meant to happen from the dawning. Each of the brothers of Newearth will leave the garden one by one. You are the oldest, so you were drawn out first."

Abriel pondered this as the next question began to form in his mind. He wondered how he could both choose his path, but it also be predetermined. He pushed the thought aside for another time.

"I miss seeing you. Can you bring me to the Great City so that I may see your face?"

"Yes," Oscar answered. Once more, Abriel felt a rush of excitement, but then his teacher completed his statement. "But not until you have completed your task."

"Oh."

"Do you remember what you are meant to do?"

"Yes," Abriel replied.

"Repeat it to me so that we may be sure,"

"I am to go to the great mountain and find a single flower. I am to give it a name and help it grow," Abriel said.

"Very good."

"But, Teacher, I do not know the way to the mountain."

"Yes, it is time for you to meet your guide. I will show you how to find him," Oscar's voice said.

Abriel smiled as he imagined the great creature that his teacher had prepared for him. He thought of the enormous brachiosaurus that had helped Oscar build the garden.

"I am ready," said Abriel.

"He is not far. You must walk toward the tree behind you and beyond."

Abriel turned and saw the tree that his teacher spoke of. He began to walk tentatively. The thick forestation made it a slow process. He pushed vines aside as he worked his way through the underbrush. He was not sure how far he was supposed to walk, but he assumed that Oscar would tell him when he arrived.

As Abriel pressed through, he saw that the light was growing more bright with each step. *There must be a clearing up ahead*, Abriel thought. He weaved his way through the low hanging branches. Within another few minutes he found himself on the edge of a great open plain.

He stopped at the edge of the clearing with the forest at his back. He let his eyes scan over the opening. It felt good to see the sky. The canopy had obscured his view for most of the day. What he saw before him was still wild, but it felt less chaotic. Waste high grass danced in the breeze, and golden shimmering light beamed down from the Great City overhead.

Abriel stepped into the clearing cautiously. He swirled side to side, looking for any creatures that might be his destined guide. He froze in his tracks when he heard a sound up ahead. His eyes bulged as he watched the grass in front of him.

THE GUIDE

A HEAD LIFTED ABOVE the grass. With a snort, the creature that the head belonged to stood to its full height. Abriel had never seen anything like it. Four powerful legs that were as long as he was tall flexed as the animal turned to look at Abriel. Its thick, powerful neck had a mane of hair that stuck out in tufts. The creature's head was as big as Abriel's entire body.

He could see at once that this creature was perfect for riding. Its long, strength-filled legs could carry him over land at an incredible speed. Abriel cooed with delight as he hoped. He charged forward to meet the creature.

The massive animal's eyes grew wild as Abriel approached. Something in the stare told Abriel to slow. He reduced his speed to a slow walk as he put his hand out and spoke softly.

"Hey there, I'm Abriel."

The giant four-legged beast reared up in panic. A frightful whinny escaped the animal's mouth. Another second and the creature turned and fled. His hooves pounded the ground like thunder as he made his escape.

Abriel watched with confusion. The animal was so fast that it would be impossible to catch. He followed the tree line for a few seconds and then turned into the woods and went out of sight. Abriel could hear his hooves fading away in the distance.

"I told that creature to flee; he is not your guide," Oscar's voice said.

"Teacher, how could there be a better guide than that. He was fast and able to be ridden."

"The guide I have chosen is better still. Keep going." Oscar said.

Abriel did not respond but was filled with wonder. Was it possible that there could be something even better suited as a guide for the journey? Abriel imagined what kind of animal Oscar might have prepared.

Abriel continued along the path that he had come into the clearing on. He walked across happily until he entered the forest on the other side of the grassy plain.

The forest there was filled less with trees and more with low-lying bushes and shrubs. The change of scenery was nice, but Abriel found it difficult to move through the smaller plants at the rate he had been going. Slower still, he continued on his journey.

After another long stretch of walking, Abriel noticed a change beginning to take place in the plant life. The trees thinned out until the ground was only covered in large leafy green patches of ivy. Still, Abriel continued.

He noticed that the ground was beginning to take on a different kind of quality. He reached down out of curiosity and found it soft, wet and squishy. Like much on his journey so far, the change filled him with questions. He had never seen proper mud before, but he relished the cool feel between his fingers. He pressed his toes in as well, and giggled at the marvelous sensation. After playing for a few minutes with the new magical substance he remembered his task. He kept walking.

As the day was drawing to a close, he came to something that seemed totally unique. During his entire life, he had only ever seen enough water to fill a leaf. In the garden, the boys gained enough moisture from the fruits they ate and the dew that gathered on the leaves.

What stood in front of him took a long few moments to comprehend. At first, he thought it was a piece of the sky that had broken off and fallen to the ground. A smooth surface of blue stretched out for a few hundred paces in front of him. When he saw ripples dance across its surface, he realized that it must be water.

He stared in amazement as the pond shimmered in the evening light. He had never seen so much water in one place. It was almost unimaginable. He ran toward the shore of the little lake with excitement. He stepped into it with utter amazement. For a few seconds, he splashed and played in the fluvial playground. Liquid enjoyment sloshed and gushed around him as he did what any boy might do. He wished his garden brothers were there. He imagined how he would splash them when their back was turned.

A strange sound caught his attention. Repeated blasts of rushing air rumbled around him. He glanced at the water; it even rippled with the gush of wind. Abriel turned to see what caused the massive sound. An enormous shadow cast itself along the water and the shore nearby.

Coming down from the open sky was the biggest bird Abriel had ever seen. Its wingspan looked to be almost half as wide as the pond itself. He squatted at the edge of the water to watch the elegant animal come in for a landing. It glided down with wings outstretched in a wide spiral. It left rippling tracks in the water as it touched down in the middle of the pond.

Abriel watched with elation as his gratitude welled up within. The bird was big enough to carry him to the mountain with ease. *This creature could carry me to the Great City itself,* Abriel thought. The bird flapped once more as it came down to float in the lake.

He stood and began to make his way across the water. The water was chest high before the bird was aware of Abriel's presence. One of its sideways eyes caught sight of him wading out. It spun toward him. Abriel's experience with the steed gave him pause. He froze where he was and let the bird get acquainted with him. This time it was the bird that did the talking.

Abriel covered his ears as the bird let out the most ear-splitting quack. He could feel the water vibrating around him with the cacophonous trumpeting. The booming blast made Abriel stumble back into the pond. Even as he moved away from the bird, it continued to bellow. He crab crawled backwards to get away from the beaked beast.

Within seconds, Abriel was out of the water and on the shore. Finally, the bird closed its beak and got quiet. It went back to floating aimlessly in the pond. Abriel watched it for a long moment, wondering what to do next.

"There is your guide," Oscar's voice said.

"It is a truly impressive creature," Abriel said. "But it doesn't seem to want me to get near."

"You must wake him."

"He seemed very awake to me," Abriel explained as respectfully as he could. A long pause followed. Abriel stood wondering what to do. He thought that might be all the instruction he was going to receive. If so, this was going to be an interesting exchange. Finally, Oscar's voice came again.

"Your guide is not the bird. Look closer."

Abriel glanced around, trying to see any other possible guide. He was relieved to find that he didn't have to tangle with the winged beak blaster, but he could not see anything that remotely resembled another creature. There were plants all around, but no other animals.

"Down." Came the teacher's voice again.

Abriel looked toward his feet.

"I don't see anything."

"Look closer," Oscar said.

Not knowing what else to do, Abriel squatted down and began to look along the muddy shore of the pond. He stayed in his kneeling position as he responded.

"All I see is this rock," Abriel said as he reached down and pulled the rock from the mud. It fit in his hand nicely. It was a half-rounded shape with a strange texture.

"That is your guide," Oscar said. Abriel glanced at the enormous bird still floating in circles in the pond.

"Are you sure?"

"Quite sure," Oscar responded. "I picked him out myself."

Abriel stared at the little lump of stone in his hand. He had assumed that his guide would be something living. He could not remember if he had been told so or not. He turned the stone over in his hand trying to understand the mystery.

He could not see how a handful of muddy rock was going to guide him to the mountain. Abriel lifted the rock toward his face to get a better look. When nothing occurred to him, he sniffed it. It smelled like what he thought a muddy rock should smell like.

Not sure what to do, Abriel reached out with his other hand and thumped the rock with his finger. To his surprise, it didn't sound like a rock. It sounded partially hollow. He tapped it again in a different place. Once more, he gave it a rapping.

Without any kind of warning, the rounded top of the rock rose up a little from his hand. Where the half dome met his palm, there was a gap in the stone. Out of the gap came a little protrusion. Abriel's eyes widened as a tiny head sprang forward.

Abriel thrust the finger he had thumped the rock with toward the little head. To his surprise, a little mouth opened up and clamped down on his finger. Impulsively, he dumped his palm toward the ground, but the little mouth held on to his poor digit.

He lifted his hand with the creature clinging to it up in front of his face. It was no rock, although he didn't know what it was. As he watched, four little legs pushed out from other openings in the hard surface, then a little tail.

The critter still clung to his finger. He marveled at it, although his finger was starting to sting. The relentless critter sank its jaw deeper into Abriel's finger tip. He wasn't sure what to do.

"He doesn't like to be lifted," Oscar's voice said.

Abriel lowered the creature to the ground immediately, and to his relief found that it let go as soon as it was back in the mud. Abriel rubbed his finger tip which was now very red. The pain was mild enough that he could overlook it.

Abriel was not sure what to do. He thought there must have been some type of misunderstanding. He knelt down lower so that he could look at the creature up close. The little guy just stared back.

"In the former world, he would have been called a turtle," Oscar's voice explained. "His name is Thunderfoot. There is no guide greater than he."

Still, Abriel could not understand how this could be the guide that Oscar had chosen. This turtle, as Teacher had called it, had legs the length of one of Abriel's fingers. He probably couldn't move more than a few paces per hour.

"Am I supposed to carry him?" Abriel asked.

"He does not like to be lifted, as you previously discovered."

"It will take years to get anywhere with Thunderfoot leading. Is there no other guide that would be more suited to the task? It is impossible for him to go so far and not be carried." Abriel said, trying to keep a respectful tone.

"All tasks are impossible until they are not," Oscar said. Abriel let a long pause follow before he responded. He felt as if he had been tricked. He did not think his teacher would mislead him, but he failed to see the logic in Thunderfoot as a guide.

"I agreed to do the task so that I could visit the Great City. It will be many years before the task is completed if Thunderfoot is my guide. Are you trying to keep me from visiting?"

"You are mistaken, my student. The Great City is not a prize for completing the journey. The journey is a reward within itself. You agreed to take the task because it was the task prepared for you before the foundations of this world were ever laid. You are not here to be served by this world but to serve it." Oscar said.

Abriel felt for the first time like his teacher was no longer teaching him, but instead saying things in order to be confusing. Abriel tried to comprehend the words that Oscar had spoken, but before he could, he spoke again.

"I will leave you with this paradox, my student. It is true that I will take you to the Great City. Yet you will never in your life visit the Great City," his voice said, and then went silent.

Abriel felt like he had fallen out of a tree and lost his breath. His stomach turned as if something were stirring his guts into a twirling storm. Oscar had told him that he would be allowed to visit the Great City. He now told him he would not.

A dark thought crept slow and heavy over the garden of his mind. Shadowy spaces in the corner of his intellect swirled. A single question brewed hot and acrid in the turmoil of his emotions.

He slowed his thoughts as the teacher had taught him to do. He fought back the indignation that boiled at the pit of his gut. He whispered the words into the air.

"This world is not the place I thought it was."

IT'S TIME

"THE FIRST OF THE twelve sons has crossed the hedge, as you know," Oscar said. Light emanated from the star-born celestial he was talking to. The great golden hall in which they met was one of many in the Holy City. Oscar waited for Yinsal to respond. The race of star-born were rarely in a hurry since they were able to straddle time. The booming voice that came from the body of burning light made Oscar feel warm.

"The foretold crossing of the man-child.
Another world born to order from wild.
Drawn he forth over hedge by calling.
To rise or endure once more a world falling."

These were the types of cryptic statements Oscar had come to expect from any of his interactions with star-born celestials. Their ability to see through time made their declarations difficult to understand. It was as if the order in which the words were said had no meaning to one of them. Oscar felt the tingle of excitement with the mystery of the prophetic utterance. It was yet another thing to be overjoyed about.

Oscar imagined Abriel making his way toward the goal he had been given. He could not believe that twelve years had already passed on Newearth. He had known that this day would come, but he did not know how short the time would feel. Time in the Holy City passed much differently than it did on the surface of the green planet. It felt like just yesterday that Oscar had taken his first trip down to the new world.

"What is to be done now that Abriel's mission has begun?" Oscar said to Yinsal. Another long pause followed as the glowing figure prepared to speak. Oscar wondered how many points in the times space continuum Yinsal was currently intersecting. The pause seemed strange considering that Yinsal probably knew what Oscar was going to say before Oscar did.

"It is time to release the tempter of twisted light.

To the world of fire take wearily your heavy flight.

Release his false gleam upon the unborn New Earth.

So that in resisting, the world may have first birth."

Oscar felt an almost palpable pressure as the weight of the instructions rested on his shoulders. He had heard of the world of fire, but never had he considered that it might be possible to go there. If he understood, and he was sure he did, he had business at the outer reaches of the universe. He felt concern as he envisioned what he might meet in that blazing cosmic horizon. He pushed the vision from his mind as he formed another question.

"If the tempter of twisted light prevails, will all be lost for Newearth?" Oscar asked.

"No thing lacks a looping purpose cycling infinitely.

For naught is lost in this, the past, or the to-be.

Whether to fire, or to light, the story now will begin.

For the sake of Him, who is forever and beyond, amen."

Oscar knew from experience that when a star-born said the word "amen," it meant the conversation was over. He had so many more questions. *How am I supposed to get to the World of Fire?* He thought. It rode the horizon of the rapidly expanding universe. No world-born celestial could pass beyond the tidal wave of creation. The ribbon of creation was constantly expanding outward at the fringed edges of the cosmos. Oscar wasn't sure if even a star-born celestial was able to cross the outer event horizon.

Without another word, Yinsal's light vanished, and Oscar was alone in the great golden hall. He turned slowly and began to walk toward the exit as he pondered. He looked to the floating orbs of light that mingled gracefully around the upper stratospheric ceiling of the chamber. His steps echoed off the distant walls.

He passed slowly toward the massive doorway he had come in through. As he exited the front of the great golden hall, he stood for a long moment on the steps. His pupils adjusted to the beaming light that the Holy City emitted constantly.

He let his eyes wander across the expanse that stretched out before him. The City was a work of art to behold. The home of the King and His people was more than Oscar had ever dreamt it could be. It was more than a city, it was a kingdom unto itself. It acted as a center point to all the inhabited worlds across the entire cosmos.

Since the end of the era of the first Earth, Oscar had visited most of the inhabited worlds. He had seen the vast floating oceans of Elantrius. He had watched the people of Saphron dance along the golden shafts of star light. He had even ventured as far as the Orresioun Belt where gravity was still young. All of these places enjoyed the benevolent rulership of the Great Cosmic King.

There was only one place that was free of the reign of the Holy City and its loving autocrat. The rumor was that it rode the wave of dark energy beyond the ribbon of nonexistence. It was to that one autonomous world that Oscar was instructed to go. He knew he needed help. Instinctively, he prayed to his King.

"My King, how am I to get there?" Oscar whispered into the air.

A flash of light and sound crackled in front of Oscar as a blueish green glow erupted and flickered. Out of the flash, a woman materialized. The spark of light was from a spacetime jump, and was not all that uncommon. The woman was shorter than Oscar and stood facing the other direction. She had materialized only centimeters from him, and apparently was unaware that he was standing closely behind her.

Oscar stepped back to give himself some room. The woman must have heard his footsteps because she turned around with a startle. She jumped as her surprise gave way to a giggle. Oscar didn't speak but just watched her as she smoothed her hair.

She had the look of one who paid very little attention to her appearance. She wore glasses, which was peculiar considering every Elvangaleen, whether resurrected or pure born had perfect vision. She continued to giggle with a slight tone of embarrassment as she put out her hand in greeting.

"My apologies, I jumped from-" she was saying but then paused. She looked at her wrist where there was nothing but skin. "I just jumped from somewhere." She continued while looking around quite confused.

"Hello, I'm Oscar."

"Ah, yes. Drexton," she said.

"No, Oscar," he corrected.

"Oscar? No, I'm pretty sure I jumped here from Drexton." She paused, then said, "Oscar, that sounds familiar. Where is it located?"

"No, Oscar is my name," he explained.

"Oh, I see." She glanced around as if something else was on her mind. She said his name a few times as if only speaking idly. "Oscar. Oscar. Oscar." Her eyes continued to wander. She surveyed the Great City around them. "Oh! Oscar. You're who I'm looking for."

"You're looking for me?" he asked.

"Yes, I came from Drexton to see you." She spun around and took in a full panoramic view of the City.

"Well, that's quite-"

"The thing is, I don't know where I am. I meant to land in the directory and find out which foundation and sector your estate is in. I'm quite confused as to how I landed here." She continued to look around.

"I was just asking the King for guidance and then you appeared," Oscar said jokingly. The woman turned toward him and gave him her full attention.

"Yes, that is it. He must have led me to you," the woman said. As if she finally remembered her manners, she reached out her hand and introduced herself. "I'm Ruth."

Oscar shook her hand and looked her in the eyes. She had a friendly demeanor with a warm, inviting smile. She looked him up and down quickly and shook her head. A tuft of hair bounced loose from the disheveled ponytail it had been tied into.

"Is something wrong?" Oscar asked.

"Do you not have a jump cloak?" Ruth asked.

"I do. I don't carry it because I don't make long jumps very often. I've only jumped between here and Newearth for the last 12 cycles or so."

"Well, you will need it today. We are going as far as far can go," she replied.

"Where are we going?"

"To the World Of Fire, Silly Dung Beetle," she said, as she took her index finger and tapped him three times in the middle of his forehead. She was definitely a strange bird, but he liked her spunk. After a moment, his fascination at her strange mannerisms were sucked into the gravity of what she just said.

WHICH WAY

ABRIEL WATCHED AS THUNDERFOOT took off in a certain direction. The little turtle was impossibly slow. Every step was a monumental achievement for the little guy. Abriel followed closely behind for a short time but quickly grew impatient. It was going to take a lifetime to get anywhere at the speed they were moving.

Abriel racked his brain for ways to speed up the progress. The little critter had reacted poorly to being picked up. Abriel's finger still stung from that lesson. Even so, he thought the most efficient way to travel would be with Thunderfoot on his shoulder. He tried to imagine a way for the turtle to signal him which direction to go.

"It'd be so much easier if I just carried you," Abriel said.

The turtle had no reaction. He simply worked on his next step at a glacial speed. Abriel huffed and sat down next to a tree. He decided that he could get off his feet and wait for Thunderfoot to make some progress. He could easily catch up after the turtle had moved any substantial distance at all.

Abriel settled in for a few minutes' rest. It felt good to sit, being that he had been standing around waiting for most of the day. As soon as he plopped down, he glanced at Thunderfoot. To his surprise, the turtle had stopped all forward motion. Abriel had to watch for a few seconds to make sure he wasn't just moving more lethargically than before. Sure enough, the turtle was sitting still.

"Why did you stop?" he asked.

Thunderfoot craned his tiny neck around and looked at Abriel. He was not familiar enough with turtle facial expressions to determine if it was a glare.

"Go on, I'll catch up," Abriel said, a little annoyed. He gestured to the turtle, trying to get him to understand. "Go on," he said again with a wave of the hand. The little shelled critter did nothing but stare. They stayed locked in a battle of glares for a few long seconds before Abriel gave in.

Again, he let out a frustrated sigh. He leaned forward and pushed off from the tree. He stomped his feet heavier than he needed to as he moved quickly, something the turtle was incapable of doing.

Once again, Thunderfoot began to take another creeping step. As dawdling as it was, at least it was progress.

When Abriel saw that the turtle had finally understood him, he sat back down next to the tree. This time, he closed his eyes, thinking he'd earned a quick nap. He thought he'd rest for a few minutes while Thunderfoot gained some ground.

With his eyes closed, he expected to hear the turtle rustling through the underbrush and leaves. He heard nothing, so he opened his eyes again. To his extreme annoyance, he found that Thunderfoot was staring at him once more. It was as if his little beady eyes were saying, "get up, you lazy bones." He let his mood get the best of him as he grumbled.

"Go on, Thunderfoot, I'll catch up."

Still, no comprehension was present on his little green face. Abriel stood quickly this time, realizing that the turtle was incapable of understanding what he was trying to do. Abriel marched forward in the direction that Thunderfoot had been going. Instead of stopping to wait for the turtle to pick up his plodding pace, Abriel breezed on past.

Within two steps, Abriel had outpaced him. He did not stop there, though. He continued on about ten paces. He figured that the turtle could catch up with him. It was obvious from Thunderfoot's path which direction they were supposed to be traveling in. Abriel plopped down beside another tree directly in the line of sight of the little stubborn beast.

To his satisfaction, the turtle continued in his direction. Abriel cheered inwardly as he watched the little stagnant critter's crawl. He finally was able to rest his eyes as Thunderfoot moved slothfully forward.

He closed his eyes and thought of the garden. He imagined what the other boys might be doing. Isod was probably chasing some poor tree dweller. Abriel laughed slightly as he watched it play out in his mind. Eduk was, no doubt, naming some new breed of berry bush he'd found. The vision filled him with warm feelings.

He realized as he sat there that he missed the smell of the garden. He wished he could be there again. More than anything, he missed his friends. He had taken them for granted. He never knew that it was possible he'd never see them again. The notion made his stomach tighten. Would he really never see them again? The thought gave him a strange feeling that he wasn't used to.

He opened his eyes, trying to escape the odd emotion. This time, he almost welcomed the distraction. He glanced over, trying to see his guide's shell. It took him a second to understand what he was looking at. Where he expected to see the turtle's head, he saw its tail. The turtle was still moving, but it was now moving in the other direction.

"What are you doing now?" Abriel grunted. Thunderfoot stopped and looked back at him. That same senseless face watched his. "Have you lost your mind? You are undoing what little progress we have made." Thunderfoot did nothing but stare. "You're going in the wrong direction!" He was becoming very put out.

It was clear what was expected. The turtle waited for him to rise and rejoin the journey. Still, Abriel breathed out his frustration on his little mindless guide.

"We were going this way, why have you turned around?"

Abriel stood reluctantly. He wondered if the turtle was playing games with him. Most played by running and frolicking, but who's to say this wasn't what running looked like for a turtle? He wondered what the teacher was thinking, pairing him with such a poorly matched guide. Abriel walked back toward the turtle as he complained.

"Some guide you are," Abriel said, but then added, "You have no idea where we are going, do you?"

He towered over the turtle with his hands on his hips. He waited as if Thunderfoot would respond. The little creature tilted its head up toward Abriel and looked at him for a few seconds. He then put his head back down and slowly began to turn in a new direction. One incredibly sluggish step at a time, the little green critter blazed a trail.

Seeing the new direction, Abriel threw his hands in the air as if there was someone there to see.

"Fine," Abriel said as he gave in and followed at a ridiculously slow pace. "I'm never going to get to see the Great City," he mumbled.

PREPARE FOR FIRE

Oscar felt the solid ground of a world under his feet, but he was momentarily disoriented. He had done a number of spacetime jumps before, but he had never gone so far in a single blast. As the bluish green light that carried him began to fade, his stomach threatened to make him sick.

He instinctively placed his hand against his abdomen as he looked around. Ruth, the woman who had come to retrieve him, was there, but now he stood in the midst of a circle of nine different individuals. He quickly surveyed the world to which they had jumped.

It was a rocky lifeless mass of lumps and dust. He looked around and noticed that the desolate scene was lit only by starlight. Craters marked the dry deserted world. Oscar had visited his fair share of lifeless planets, but never had much cause to spend any time on one. He was a gardener and teacher by trade. Although the trip was interesting so far, the adventure left him feeling a little confused.

Taking a deep breath, he sensed that the air was different. He pulled a full lung full and speculated that it had little or no oxygen. It seemed to sit in his lungs like a heavy, wet garment. He decided to make his breathing minimal.

He glanced around the circle of individuals that were arrayed around where he and Ruth had landed. Looking at each one, he found that he had not seen any of them before. Along with Ruth, there was another man who looked to be world-born. That was, however, not what had his attention.

Standing in formation nearby was a platoon of seven enormous star-born celestials. Their skin radiated light as would polished gold. He glanced at them quickly. Even with his regular interactions with star-born beings, he never quite got used to being in their presence. He admired their powerful stature for a moment longer than he intended to.

The small audience of nine stared at him as if he were supposed to speak. He wasn't sure what to say. He knew very little about why he was there. He knew he had prayed to the King for guidance, but he didn't know how this would connect to that situation. He knew he needed to get to the World of Fire, but he wasn't sure how.

"I am not sure-" he started to say, but cut his words off short. His voice was about an octave lower than he had expected. It sounded like his voice had been recorded and then slowed down to about half speed. He put his hand to his throat and tried again. "Something is wrong with my voice. It's lower."

"The atmosphere is comprised of Sulfur Hexafluoride. It's much heavier than a livable atmosphere. Your voice will sound strange to your ears, but you will get used to it," said the other world-born man. Ruth had taken her position next to him. It was clear that they were companions. Although Oscar had never heard the man's voice before, it too seemed much lower than it should.

"I see," Oscar said. He suppressed a giggle on account of the seriousness of the mission. It would take time to get used to his new voice.

"I am Truss," the man said as he reached out and hugged Oscar. Oscar returned the gesture. "I hear you are the Newearth teacher."

"Yes," Oscar said. "The time of the tempting is almost here. I can't believe how fast it has happened."

Truss looked back at Oscar with a slight smile. He regarded him for a moment. Oscar felt a kind of brotherly bond with the man. Truss was about to say something, but

Ruth blurted out in a voice that was far too low for her miniature stature.

"Truss is a world builder. The King used him to build Newearth." Ruth's voice was comical, but Oscar did not laugh. He was taken by the statement. Truss put his hand on Ruth's shoulder as if to keep her from bragging on him anymore. He smiled as he spoke.

"It was a concert of talents. Praise the King that he gave us the tools to craft it," Truss said with his eyes on Ruth. The bond between these two new friends made Oscar feel warm. They all stood there for another moment.

"Newearth is truly beautiful. I'm quite fond of it," Oscar said with a smirk. The low timbre of his voice made it feel more important somehow.

Without meaning to, Oscar glanced at the huge star-born figures standing only paces away. They could have been statues of pure gold for all he knew. They were completely still. Truss took the cue.

"Ahh, my apologies. I have not introduced you to the team," Truss said as he gestured with an open hand toward the mammoth celestials. Oscar turned toward them. They each had to be at least twice his height. If he were close enough, he was pretty sure he could see his own reflection in their skin.

"Sir," Oscar said as he nodded a greeting toward the giant.

"Greetings, redeemed one." The voice that came from the premier celestial was like thunder. Oscar could feel the vibration in his feet. It rumbled through his chest like a mighty wind. He wasn't sure if the sound was augmented by the heavy atmosphere, but it was truly something powerful to hear. Oscar tried to respond but found himself short of words, so the golden celestial spoke again.

"General Zath is how I am called, and these six are my trusted," the massive juggernaut said. Oscar found it difficult to look into the face of the powerful, statuesque figure. He only nodded as his eyes involuntarily flitted to the ground. Oscar turned back toward Truss and Ruth, trying to release himself from the impossible conversation he was failing to have.

Truss stepped forward and gave a friendly slap on Oscar's back. He was thankful for the distraction. Ruth stepped in close as if she knew what was about to happen. Oscar looked at the two faces. He wondered why he was allowed to associate with such impressive company.

"May I ask why we are here?" Oscar said, but then added, "And where here is?"

Truss pulled something from a hidden pocket in his cloak. Oscar recognized it at once, although it had been a long time since he'd seen one. Between Truss' fingers, he gripped a hand-carved pencil. His other hand pressed into a pocket, and from it he produced a small notebook.

Something about it made Oscar feel at home. Truss opened to an empty page and began to sketch as he spoke. Oscar noticed that Truss did not look at the page as he drew. The perfectly contoured lines built into a resplendent piece of art on the page.

"Here we are on Drexton," Truss said as his hand traced out a perfect sphere on the textured paper. He drew in an array of constellational points. "Drexton is near the outer edge of the created universe." Truss sketched a jagged line that encompassed the entire page. He shaded it to look something like the membrane of a bubble.

"At the outer edge is the ribbon of light," Truss said. Oscar had heard the term before, but never quite understood what it meant. It had been described to him as the outside wall of the universe. Oscar saw an opportunity to gain a deeper understanding, so he asked.

"What is the ribbon of light?" Oscar said. Truss seemed to light up with the question. He kept his finger on the page he was working on, but turned to a new one to make a fresh drawing. The sketch was so vibrant as it took shape that Oscar could almost see colors in the monochromatic scrawl.

"The ribbon of light is the Primary Directive. It is the ever-expanding word of the King. The original word," Truss said as if it made any sense. His hand continued to draw as Oscar looked up at his face. Oscar adequately expressed his confusion, so Truss continued.

"The Primary Directive of the King was, 'let there be.' It is the spark of creation. The ribbon of light is the ever-expanding tidal wave of creation energy that moves outward from the original singularity." Truss said as he penciled a heavy center point on the page. He tapped it with his finger as he continued.

"Creation was not one single event that took place in the past. It is a continual expanding occurrence that is always happening. It happens at the outer spherical belt of the cosmos where the something is touching the nothing." Truss flipped back to the previous page where he had drawn the curved ribbon across the paper.

"It is the living boundary of the universe. It is constantly gaining ground and moving away from us, making the universe ever bigger every second," Ruth added.

He felt like his brain had just been twisted around three times inside his skull. He had no idea that these things were possible. Truss continued as Oscar tried to wrap his brain around the concept.

"The ancients from your world noticed this phenomenon. They saw with tiny optic devices that the universe was expanding quickly, but they could not understand the equations because they were missing variables. They called these unknown variables dark energy and dark matter." Truss now wrote numbers and equations across the bottom of the page. His hand moved so quickly that Oscar could barely keep up with his eyes.

"What they didn't understand was that the ribbon of light introduces new energy and matter into the universe as it ripples outward from the source point. They thought that the inception of the universe was one singular big bang." Truss drew arrows radiating out from the center point of the page.

"They saw the ribbon of light but didn't know what it was. They thought it was leftover radiation from that singular event, instead of activity that was constantly happening. The equation becomes balanced when you consider the variable of continual creation, instead of single point action," Truss said as he added a few numbers to the equation at the bottom of the page.

Oscar looked at him, stunned. He was no mathematician, but he generally grasped the concept. His eyes jolted from Truss to Ruth and back to the page. Oscar could hardly think straight; his mind was racing so quickly. It was turning out to be a very interesting day.

"Pretty swell, huh?" Ruth said. He nodded but then added another question to the growing pile of mystery.

"I was told that nothing could ever reach the ribbon of light, because it moves so fast," Oscar said, letting his tone imply the question. Truss responded.

"Yes, that's right. The speed of light itself is based on the speed of the ribbon. So we would never be able to reach the ribbon with conventional methods. We can't jump past it because there is no space-time beyond to jump to. We can't jump to it, because by the time we are there, it will be gone," he said.

"It's like hitting a moving target, but in this case, the target is moving at light speed," Ruth added.

It felt like they were setting up an impossible situation just so they could wow him with the solution.

"What's more, the World of Fire sits beyond the edge of the created universe. It rides the tidal wave of the ribbon of light. It is suspended in the void. Not even space exists beyond that point."

Oscar stepped back from the conversation and rubbed his hand on his chin. He could not see the solution, but he knew there must be one. He had been given instructions to go to the World of Fire. He realized that he was in over his head. He didn't understand the forces at play. He was as close to scared as an Elvangaleen could be.

"Is there a way? I am supposed to go to the World of Fire," Oscar said with a note of defeat in his voice.

"I will provide the passage," came the booming voice of General Zath. The rumbling tone startled Oscar. As he jumped he turned to look at Zath. His burnished aesthetic awed him as he let his eyes follow the lines of the statue like creature. *Of course,* he thought, *why else would a star-born be needed.*

"General Zath will create a tesseract arc through the ribbon of light. He will tie the tesseract to the gravity of this world so that we will be able to return. Through the tesseract, we will be able to exist within the World of Fire for a short time," Truss said.

Oscar was seeing the pieces falling into place. Only minutes before he had been in the Holy City wondering how he was going to fulfill his mission. Now the answer stood right here in front of him. As he looked to each of the characters that were about to play a role in this great epic a singular question arose in his mind.

"Is it possible that we will fail, or worse?" he asked to no one in particular. It was Ruth who answered in her low-pitched, alien voice.

"Failure is always an option, but that's what makes it fun." He was surprised at her strange, lighthearted candor. He wondered what she must have gone through to feel that way about going to the World of Fire.

Oscar saw himself as small and inexperienced next to these great figures of courage and strength. This would be a day to remember, if he made it out of the World of Fire. He had to consider the possibility that something could go wrong. He whispered a silent prayer.

"My King, be with us as we enter-" He trailed off as he looked into the starlit sky. Somewhere out there was the torrid flame-covered world that rode the tidal wave of light. He could barely bring himself to whisper its proper name. Quieter this time, he whispered it as chills tickled his spine.

"My King, be with us as we enter Hell."

GETTING STUCK

AFTER FOLLOWING THUNDERFOOT FOR a day and a half, Abriel was getting very tired of his extremely slow pace. He had tried everything he could think of to speed the little turtle up, but nothing worked.

Picking Thunderfoot up inevitably meant Abriel would get his finger or hand bitten. The longer he held him, the harder the critter would bite. He had tried talking Thunderfoot into a faster route. He had even considered things more radical, but it was no use. His little shelled guide was either as stubborn as they come or completely oblivious to Abriel's plight.

After looking at it from every angle he could, Abriel decided that there must have been a mistake. He was almost certain that he had misunderstood what Oscar had wanted him to do. It was impossible for the teacher to want him to continue at this speed. He had a job to do after all.

He tried to convince himself that completing the task was his only motivation, but sneaking around in the back of his mind, he could see that there was more to it. In reality, he was still thinking about his promised trip to the Holy City.

He had made no progress in understanding the paradox that Teacher had given him about the future trip, but he felt confident that it would work itself out. That is, it would work out if he ever made it to the mountain and found this mysterious flower. Abriel was beginning to think that it would never happen.

He stared down at Thunderfoot, who was having a particularly hard time navigating himself over an ordinary twig. He watched as Thunderfoot became high-centered on the little stick. As he had done many times that day, Abriel squatted down to help the little creature step over the obstacle. The turtle's shell rode so low to the ground that even mildly uneven terrain left him immobile.

As he reached his hand out to help Thunderfoot, something gave him pause. He looked at his little green shell, his inadequate legs, and his little bobbing head. As far as Abriel could tell, the turtle didn't even realize he was stuck. He probably thought he was still moving forward.

"You're stuck," Abriel said, instead of helping him. The turtle's eyes glanced slightly upward in Abriel's direction.

He made no change in action as his little legs continued to scramble without purchase.

"Do you even know that you're stuck?" Abriel asked. Still no response.

Without touching him, Abriel stood to his full height and looked out at the wild forest around. He would be as likely to find the great mountain on his own. *In fact,* he thought, *I would probably find the mountain more quickly if I didn't have to look out for this little pitiful creature.*

The thought swelled in his mind. Maybe that was the point of this lesson. Maybe the teacher was expecting him to realize that he didn't need help. Abriel puffed his chest a little as he imagined himself striking out on his own. He reveled in the adventurous thought of a solo journey. Wouldn't the teacher be that much more proud of him if he did it alone?

"I think I'll go," Abriel said. "I can move more quickly by myself." Thunderfoot didn't indicate that he heard him. He continued to kick his little feet without avail.

It occurred to Abriel that the turtle might have just been leading him in circles since yesterday. Thunderfoot gave no hint that he had a clue what was going on. The cranky little beast was insufferable, and Abriel had had enough.

He looked around again as if waiting for permission, but nothing happened. Since there was no direct instruction to stay, Abriel assumed he could do as he pleased. So he did. He picked a direction, which happened to be the same direction Thunderfoot was trying for. It looked like a good path as far as he could tell.

He told himself not to look back. He was so tired of following the slowest creature on Newearth that he didn't even want to know what the little guy was doing. As he stepped away, he could feel his stride growing. He could sense his feet getting faster. With each stride, his gait increased until he was running.

It felt good to run. His heart jumped into action as his legs pumped beneath him. This was freedom. He felt like he had been tied down for the last day and a half. He sped from a jog to a sprint. It was intoxicating to stretch his legs.

SWACK!

A branch or a vine or something smacked his leg hard. He didn't care. He was like a bird flying through the forest at top speed. He couldn't care less about a...

SWACK!

Another something hit his arm as he ran. He hadn't seen it, but this one smarted a little. No matter, he was so enjoying the run he could hardly-

SWACK!

Now that one got his attention. *That's going to leave a mark*, he thought. As he continued to glide effortlessly

through the forest, his gliding became less and less effort-
less as more and more obstructions whacked his skin.

One after another smacked, slapped, whacked, and wal-
loped him. He thought about slowing down. The image of
Thunderfoot caught on a branch popped into his mind.
The little critter couldn't even negotiate a twig.

"This is how it's done, Thunderfoot!" Abriel shouted as
if the turtle could hear him. He pressed his youthful body
harder as he sped up even more. As he rocketed through
the trees at near top speed he noticed things beginning to
blur by. The heart thumping excitement of it all made him
feel alive again.

In the path ahead he noticed a web of vines that were
blocking the way. Again he thought of how Thunderfoot
could get caught on the slightest of obstacles. He imagined
himself bursting through the vines like some kind of trail
blazing hero. He envisioned himself reaching the mountain by early afternoon.

As the vines and branches that blocked the passage
loomed closer, he pushed for a little more speed. His feet
pressed into the moist ground as he galloped forward. He
let his arms fly behind him as he reached the obstacle,
thinking he would bust through with his chest puffed out.

The feeling that met his skin was not what he expected.
His head jerked hard as he plowed violently into the mess

of vines and branches. He had expected to erupt through like the victor of some fantastic game. That is, however, not how it played out.

His speed carried him into the vines and allowed his body to flip backward from where he impacted. As he tumbled upside down and backwards he felt a networking orchestra of vines and limbs rake over his skin. Fortunately, he did not topple for long. Unfortunately, his forward progress was absorbed by the web of wild forest that now surrounded him.

It took him a minute to get his bearings. His head was still spinning from the impact. His legs were above his body, and one of his arms was pinned behind him. He tried to twist himself free. The weight of his body was pushing one side of his head into the dirt.

As he tried to pull his free arm around to untangle his other, he found that he could not maneuver. His first instinct was to move slowly and methodically, but being that he was upside down and very uncomfortable, that is not what he did. He used as much force as he had to try and loose his pinned hand.

The feeling of being trapped was new to him. He had not ever imagined that it was possible. The vines were of all sizes, large and small. He tried another time to pull an arm or a leg free, but it was no use. After yet another attempt he decided that he would have to think of something else to try.

He stilled his body and took a deep breath. With all his might, he flexed every muscle he could. With violent resolve, he pushed in every direction possible. Looking for anything to budge, he continued his wild struggle for a few seconds but found himself more stuck than he already was.

At one point, he was able to get his free hand down around his ankle. Thinking he would free his foot, he thrust his hand through the loop that held it. Without meaning to, he had sprung a tighter trap still. The new loop around his formerly free wrist tightened as it pulled through a narrow set of others. Now his entire body was snared in an impossible trap of wiry plant life.

He felt his head getting heavy with the rush of blood. He was still breathing deeply from his run. His face was getting hot, and his legs were beginning to tingle from lack of circulation. He grunted as he made another attempt at freedom.

He had never felt totally powerless before, but he was quickly getting acquainted with the sensation. It was his least favorite feeling so far. With his body suspended upside down and his head twisted at an uncomfortable angle, he eased his muscles and tried to think.

He was seeing little white specks at the edge of his vision. They danced around like shooting stars. He wondered how long he could stay like this. How long was it possible to be trapped? He had never been trapped before so he wasn't sure what the rules were.

The only thing he could think to do was call for help. "Teacher," he yelled with as much volume as he could manage. His voice sounded squeezed and unnatural. "Teacher, help me."

THE TESSERACT

GENERAL ZATH PORTRAYED NO emotion as he began to open the tesseract, whatever that was. They had explained it as a multidimensional array of space, but Oscar was not sure he fully grasped the meaning. He was assuming it was something similar to a wormhole.

The glowing skin of Zath began to blaze brighter as he pressed himself through openings he made in space. Oscar watched his other star-born companions as they too were emotionless. Truss and Ruth stood close to Oscar as the space around them began to warp.

"We are close now," Zath said. His booming voice shook the ground but Oscar wasn't concerned with that. He could feel his body responding to dimensional shift in a way that he was not used to.

The light and sound around them were now bending and shifting in unfamiliar ways. Oscar tried to understand what he was seeing, but it was impossible. It was as if the layers of light were stacking up on top of each other.

Trying to shield his eyes, he held his hand in front of his face. All at once, he could see not only his skin but everything below it as well. It was as if the inside of his body was wrapped and layered on top of the outside. He felt no change in his body or hand. He turned it over. As he did it moved in a very peculiar way.

It was as if all of the parts of his hand were moving through one another. It was as if the molecules no longer moved together but were instead only being rearranged. He was mesmerized by the scene. He glanced up to see if Ruth or Truss were as surprised.

His eyes found it almost impossible to pick them out from the background. It was as if the image of the dusty planet, his new friends, and the space beyond were all transposed on top of each other. His eyes searched for meaning in the massive array of confusing beams of light.

"Welcome to the deeper dimensions," Truss said. Even his voice was not as it had been. It was as if the sound carried with it something more than just words. It was as if Oscar could sense the essence of each word that the sounds were tied to.

"Why does it look so strange?" Oscar asked. The sound of his voice was layered with the same bizarre essence that he had heard in Truss's. It was Ruth who responded this time.

"You are seeing the dimensions piling up on top of each other. That's what Zath's tesseract does. It makes it possible for us to move as the star-born do," Ruth said, although the sound of her voice was almost imperceptible. He could feel the meaning in the words. It was as if the noises that came from her mouth were not important. The meaning that drifted through him did not need the words to be expressed.

"How many dimensions are there?" Oscar asked. He felt the meaning of his own words escaping from his body, but he was not sure if he was actually speaking. Truss answered.

"The first four dimensions you know about, time being the fourth. There are not words for the dimensions below these four." Truss said.

"Can we survive passing through them?" Oscar asked wordlessly.

"Survive? You have always lived in every dimension. You are just unaware of them. Think of it as subconsciousness. Your mind is always doing basic and foundational things that you don't sense. The lower dimensions form the subconscious foundation for the upper ones that we sense. These dimensions are like the cosmos' subconscious," Truss said.

Zath pressed harder against the boundaries of the dimensional construct and began to pull deeper layers through each other. He weaved the dimensions into a spiraling vortex until the pool of space was tumultuous. He glowed white as a burning star. Oscar tried to close his eyes. The image of his eyelids superimposed over the scene of Zath and his companions. Oscar tried to distract himself from the frightening view by asking another question.

"What are the deeper dimensions?" Oscar said. He wasn't even sure if the question made sense, but he was hoping that he could hide his fear of what was happening around him.

"It is hard to put them into words. The simplest explanation would be things like meaning, logic, attraction, and repulsion. Each dimension down becomes closer to the universal binary, which is the most basic dimension: love. That's why the World of Fire must be outside the boundaries of the universe. To live inside the universe yet be out of phase with the dimensional construct is torture."

Oscar was surprised that the meaning came easily. It was not blocked and bogged down by flimsy words, but flowed into his mind without effort. He could see the value of a deeper awareness. He wondered if this was how the star-born experienced the universe.

"So the King is showing kindness to those in the World of Fire by allowing them to live outside the universe?" Oscar asked.

"That's right. Their continual rebellion against the King is torture enough, the King has given them the only kindness they have left him to give, banishing them to outer darkness is a type of mercy," Ruth said.

Oscar marveled at the meaning. He had never considered Hell to be a kindness. It was certainly judgment and condemnation, but there was a type of grace in it. Oscar could see now that for these rebels to live within the boundaries of the universe would mean they would be punished endlessly by the cosmos itself. They had rebelled not only against the King, but against the natural order of things. There was no way for them to have bliss either in the universe or outside.

"Can those who live in the World of Fire ever come back from the darkness?" Oscar asked. His heart and soul seemed to hang on the response to the question. He wanted to have hope for these lost souls. He wanted to believe that they were not truly lost.

"Yes, they are free to come back to the light, but none ever have. They need only to believe in the King, and he would rescue them from corruption, although none of them ever do. It is speculated that none ever will. They have damned themselves by wanting to be their own king, and so the true King has allowed each of the condemned to be a kingdom of his own. Living on into eternity as an autonomous country. Each has what they desired, true freedom."

The deep and haunting meaning seemed to echo through spacetime as Oscar let its essence soak into his mind. He did not know what to expect when they crossed over, but he was physically afraid. To his knowledge no world born celestial had ever done what he was about to do. He turned his attention toward the General, although he could not be sure if his eyes moved.

Zath's enormous presence seemed to spiral on into forever from where he stood. It looked as if he were simultaneously rushing forward and moving away at an incredible speed. He spoke, but his voice sounded different than it had before.

"The tesseract is nearly open," Zath said. "I will pull us all through. Do not leave the bubble that my companions create, or you may become lost."

Oscar had not yet heard that there was danger of becoming lost. He glanced downward toward his chest and saw the layer of molecules that throbbed there. It didn't feel right to call it his heart.

Something seemed to click around them. The final step must have been reached because Oscar could see in every direction at once. Not only could he see the physical matter around him, the light rays that bounced, the streams of logic, the laws of physics, but he could see the most basic fabric of the universe. The universal binary, as Truss had called it, wove through him and outward. The universe, he could now see was built on the foundational dimension of love.

He followed these interconnected lines that spider-webbed out from him to his new friends. He looked to them and saw that the glowing bond between them was stronger than the one that tied him to them. He turned his attention toward another great, bright set of threads leading away from his body. There were so many.

The web was made of woven strings of variagated colors and thicknesses. He found a set of twelve lines leading away. Although he could not see where they terminated, he could sense that they were the bonds of love for his students. They were so far away, on the other side of the universe in fact, but they glowed and crackled with the electricity of life.

The greatest and brightest tendril shot out from him like a beacon of tremendous glory. He followed the line with his mind. He knew where it led. It was tied to the center of the universe, just like every thread in the cosmic tapestry was. All these networking bonds of love radiated outward from the center of the universe, which was the great and marvelous Holy King. At the center of the dimensional construct, the King stood with all of the threads leading to him. It happened in such a flash that it was over almost as quickly as it had started.

In a fraction of a second the light was dying, the dimensions were sliding back into their invisible array. Before the image was totally gone from his mind he looked one last time to the glowing figure that stood ever closer and yet at the center of the cosmos. Although he could not speak, he uttered the essence, "My King, you are more than I ever dreamed."

The image went black. A faint glow of orange and red began to dance around them.

FREEDOM

ABRIEL WAS BEGINNING TO wonder if he would have to live out his entire life stuck upside down in a tangle of branches and vines. He had continued to try to get free, but each time he found himself more ensnared. He had hoped that calling out to his teacher would have a favorable result, but there was no response.

So he waited. His body was extremely uncomfortable from the precarious position he was in. Most of his weight was on his neck. His head was throbbing.

Being completely trapped allowed his mind to wander. He thought of the great Holy City and wondered if he had lost his chances at ever reaching it. His mind drifted to the other boys still in the garden. He wished he could go back and be a simple boy again, instead of this strange neutral zone. He was no longer a boy, but not yet a man.

He heard something crackling nearby. He opened his eyes and tried his best to look around. His range of motion was very limited, but he scanned the upside-down scene. A distance off, maybe ten or twenty paces, was a small creature moving through the underbrush. It crept painfully slow. Abriel's heart leapt. He could not see clearly, but hoped with all his heart that it was Thunderfoot.

Abriel realized how quickly his feelings had changed. Only hours earlier he had been ready to never see the little turtle again. Now it felt like the stubborn beast was his only hope. His voice came out in a broken croak.

"Thunderfoot, is that you?"

There was no reply. In fact, the creeping sound stopped completely. Abriel tried not to let it discourage him. He watched intently, hoping his suspicion was correct. He called out again.

"Thunderfoot, I'm stuck. If that's you, I could use some help."

Even if it was Thunderfoot, he was not sure what the little creeper could do to fix his predicament. Abriel was a hundred times more powerful than the turtle, so it was unlikely that Thunderfoot could help him escape.

That didn't matter, however. Even if there was nothing that Thunderfoot could do, he was still happy to have the company. His mood began to lift as he watched and waited for his little companion to emerge. It felt like hours of anticipation as he listened to the slow rustling sounds.

For all Abriel knew, it *was* hours. His guess was that this was Thunderfoot's top speed. Abriel called out to him a number of times, but as expected, there was no response.

Abriel must have dozed off because he came to it with a startle. He felt a pinch on his forehead. He opened his eyes to realize that it was nearly dark. How long had he been in this position? He tried to focus his eyes to see if Thunderfoot was nearby. Another pinch, sharper this time, bit into the skin on his forehead.

"Oww," Abriel cried loudly, more out of surprise than frustration. "Thunder, is that you?"

As best he could, Abriel pressed his head backward to give his eyes enough distance to focus. Sure enough, there the little creature stood. Finally, they were eye to eye. Thunderfoot regarded him for a long moment as Abriel stared back.

"So what do we do now?" Abriel asked. The turtle stood stone still and looked back at him. Although he was almost sure that the critter was an unthinking beast, he held out hope that Thunderfoot might have a plan to get him out of this situation.

Abriel watched as the turtle began to open his mouth. It hurt his eyes to focus so close to his face. When the turtle had his mouth open fully, he closed it again. It looked like he had taken a deep breath, but Abriel had never seen him do it before. He continued to watch as Thunderfoot did it again. He opened his mouth as wide as he could, then closed it.

"What are you doing?" Abriel asked. The turtle made no indication that he understood. A little bit quicker this time, Thunderfoot did it once more. Now with a deliberate rhythm to his jaw-dropping routine, Thunderfoot opened and closed his mouth over and over. Abriel watched. There was nothing else he could do.

After observing the turtle's behavior for a long few minutes, Abriel began to wonder if Thunderfoot was trying to communicate. His miniature jaw was moving up and down, but what could it mean?

"What are you doing?" Abriel asked again as if his little guide could simply answer. He watched another few minutes as he tried to divine some meaning from the moving mouth. Abriel was pretty sure it meant nothing, but he would grasp at any hope of an escape.

"Are you telling me to chew through the vines?" Abriel asked. He watched Thunderfoot, hoping for some reasoned response. He got none. "It's worth a try, I guess."

He turned his head as far to one side as he could. It was extremely uncomfortable, but he wanted out. There was a vine that had been sitting across Abriel's throat and chest. He squirmed his body as much as possible in order to get the vine in proper chewing position. After a few minutes of work, he was able to open his mouth just right.

With the vine between his teeth, he bit down, gently at first, to see how possible it was. The vine was spongy. With the test bite out of the way, Abriel clenched his teeth down as hard as he could. They sank into the vine as juice ran down his face and into his nose. It was not tasty, nor was it vile. He relaxed his jaw in order to bite again when he felt a familiar pinch.

Thunderfoot bit him hard on his eyebrow. Abriel immediately spat the vine from his mouth and tried to move his head back. The turtle let go and waddled back a step.

"What did you do that for?" Abriel barked. His eyebrow stung. He focused on the turtle again, hoping for an explanation. For a moment, Thunderfoot stood still, but as he watched, the turtle's mouth began to move. Abriel said, "No, not that again."

As before, the turtle stared at him as he opened and closed his mouth over and over. Thunderfoot continued this strange little ritual. Abriel was almost sure that it didn't mean anything. After a few minutes passed, Abriel decided that there was nothing more to be done. It was almost dark, so he decided to close his eyes and see if he could get some sleep.

"Ouch. What is your problem?" Abriel asked. As soon as he had closed his eyes, the turtle had clamped down on his cheek. His face was going to look like the inside of a ripe tomato before this was all over. It took a minute for the sting to wear off. Apparently, Thunderfoot was trying to communicate.

"So, you don't want me to chew through the vines, and you don't want me to go to sleep. What is it that you want me to do?" Abriel looked at the little upside-down turtle. For the briefest fraction of an instant, the turtle paused and then went back to opening and closing his mouth.

Feeling quite ridiculous, Abriel decided to simply mimic the turtle. He didn't understand how it would do any good, but he was tired of getting bit, and would try anything. So he did exactly as the turtle did. Open. Close. Open. Close. On and on his mouth went. He watched Thunderfoot. Apparently, this wasn't what he wanted either because he slunk forward and bit him again.

"Owww!" Abriel yelped. "I don't know what you want me to do," he said. Once again, Thunderfoot opened and closed his mouth rhythmically. *This turtle is out of his mind*, Abriel thought. *Is he just going to torture me like this for the rest of my life?* Something told him that wasn't the case. He sensed that there was some meaning in what the turtle was doing. He felt it, he just couldn't figure out what it was.

"We can figure this out. You want me to do something right?" At this, the turtle stopped moving his mouth. "Ahhh, you're not biting me, so that must be correct. You want me to do something, but it's not chewing through the vine." No bite. "Or going to sleep." No bite. "Or moving my mouth." This time, Thunderfoot stepped forward and bit him, but it was a gentle bite this time. It definitely felt like they were communicating now. He tried the opposite.

"So you do want me to move my mouth." Thunderfoot didn't bite him. "But I moved my mouth and you bit me." Abriel racked his brain trying to understand what it might mean. He thought he saw a spark of meaning. "Oh, you don't want me to *only* move my mouth. You want me to do something else while I move my mouth?" Finally, there was a glimmer of hope. The turtle did not bite him.

"So, what can I do while moving my mouth?" Abriel asked more to himself than to Thunderfoot. "I can talk." It occurred to him that as long as he was talking, the turtle had not bitten him. "So am I supposed to keep talking about nothing. Is that what you want me to do?" The turtle stepped forward and bit him gently. It didn't hurt.

"So you don't just want me to talk about nothing, you want me to talk about something specific?" Abriel asked. The turtle did nothing, so he assumed he was on the right track. Although he was as confused as ever.

"What do you want me to talk to you about?" Abriel asked, not expecting an answer. Once more, Thunderfoot leaned forward and bit him with a soft touch.

"You don't want me to talk to *you*?" Abriel asked. The turtle didn't respond, so he took the answer to be a 'yes'. He felt like he was getting better at understanding.

"Who do you want me to talk to? I've tried to call out to the teacher, and he did not respond. There's no one else here," Abriel said. That one earned him a bite. So he rephrased it.

"Is there someone else here?" Abriel asked. He felt like he had just unlocked an incredible puzzle. The turtle turned and began to walk away. His first instinct was to ask him what he was doing, but instead, he just watched. Thunderfoot stepped slowly over to the base of a nearby tree. Abriel had to crane his neck uncomfortably to see him.

Thunderfoot faced the tree, opened and closed his mouth a number of times, and then looked back at him. All at once, it hit him. His teacher's lessons on cultivation rushed back to him as he blurted out.

"You want me to talk to the vines." He didn't have to ask; he knew it was the answer. It was so obvious, he didn't know why he hadn't thought of it. He had been in such a hurry that he had not even thought to try what he had learned from Oscar. Without a moment's delay, he got to work.

Oscar had taught the boys that before they could cultivate, they must name the plants that are going to be worked with. From where he was, he began to look around. Most of the vines seemed to be intertwined between two main trees. The majority of the branches that drooped down low were from the two huge trunks of these trees. He glanced at the one on his right and spoke loud and proud.

"You will be called Rathbin Potifrax." He giggled with delight. He could almost forget his discomfort in light of his given task. He turned to the other main tree and nearly shouted with joy. "You are to be called Istrix Mistronia!" Although he knew the words had no meaning, it suddenly felt like these two trees could have no other name other than what he had just given them.

He let his eyes follow the main set of vines. He realized that the vines were independent of the trees, which meant they needed a name as well. Considering how long he had spent trapped by these spongy stalks, he felt like they needed a nomenclature that reflected their sly nature.

"You will be called the Deep Snare Vine," he said. He had not realized how much fun it could be to give a name. He thought back to the day in the garden when he had resisted his teacher's lesson. How could he have been so dense? This was a wild kind of fun. It felt like he had just come alive again.

It was time to begin the cultivation phase. He glanced around to see what Thunderfoot was doing. He didn't see him anywhere in sight, but he was not concerned at the moment. He set out to accomplish his goal. With a fresh delight, he imagined himself free.

"Rathbin Potifrax, you are to shed your low-hanging, west-facing branches," Abriel said to the massive tree. He hoped this would allow the vines to loosen, although he knew the tree would not be able to do it quickly.

"Istrix Mistronia, you are to shed your low hanging east facing branches." That would allow the snare to unwind easily, although he wasn't sure how long it would take for the two huge trees to follow his instructions. He hoped that the vine could react more quickly than the trees. He was sure it was a more rapid growth plant, and so he began to speak instructions to it as well.

"Deep Snare Vine, you are to grow only along the ground. You are never to grow above ground unless you are otherwise instructed. You are to shed the vines that wrap between Potifrax and Mistronia," Abriel said.

He knew that if he had done it right, it would still be hours or even days before the plants could properly release him. The trees especially were slow growing hard woods. Now that his talk was complete, all he could do now was wait.

"You were right, Thunder. I don't know why I didn't think of it," he said. Abriel looked around for Thunderfoot, but he was not in sight. "Thunder, where did you go?"

The little turtle was such a mystery. He was as slow as the seasons, but somehow he had slipped away. Abriel was confident that Thunderfoot had not abandoned him. Because he could do nothing else, he waited.

As the nighttime hours passed, Abriel's stomach began to grumble. He had rarely ever felt hunger. Once or twice, he had woken in the morning after a long night's sleep with a belly begging for food. While he lived in the garden, it was easy to fill his stomach on berries, nuts, or fruit.

It had not occurred to Abriel that he might have to endure hunger while trapped between Potifrax and Mistronia. Another louder rumble came from his stomach. It was growing in intensity.

"Thunder, are you around here somewhere?" Abriel called out. The silence that followed was hollow and eerie. Was it possible that Abriel was all alone again? It didn't make sense. Why would his little guide show up to help him get free, only to disappear once more?

In the dark, Abriel waited. He was still excited from using the lessons that the teacher had given him, so he couldn't sleep. He kept his eyes open, hoping to catch sight of his friend.

After another few minutes, Thunderfoot emerged from behind a shrubby bush about five paces away. In his mouth was something Abriel did not recognize.

As the turtle approached, Abriel wondered what the little mysterious guide was up to. When he was face to face with him, Abriel saw that the thing in his mouth was a long green stalk. Abriel wasn't sure what it was, but he quickly got the idea.

Thunderfoot sidestepped and craned his neck up so that the green stalk reached just up to Abriel's mouth. Thankful for the generosity, Abriel opened wide and stretched his lips out to take a bite of the green plant.

He had never tasted anything so wonderful. He had meals that were probably more tasty, but he had never eaten before when he was this hungry. Somehow, the hunger intensified the experience. He gulped down the stalk bite by bite. Once that one was finished, Thunderfoot waddled off again.

It was slow, but one by one, the turtle brought Abriel an entire meal's worth of food. Ground cabbage, big juicy leaves, even a root that Abriel had never tasted before. It was difficult to swallow upside down but he was extremely thankful for his little friend.

Abriel beamed with joy on the inside. Thunderfoot had turned out to be more than he could have possibly dreamed. Abriel was convinced. This creature was the perfect guide; Abriel had just been too much in a hurry to notice.

Although he was not free yet, he could almost swear that the vines were beginning to loosen.

A WORLD ON FIRE

AN ORANGE GLOW SURROUNDED Oscar. The tesseract jump left him disoriented for a second, but he quickly regained composure. He squinted, trying to see his surroundings. His eyes began to adjust to the lower light conditions.

Dimly lit columns of smoke rose up into the space over his head. What little light was visible was choked by the falling ash and soot that drifted through the atmosphere.

The heat was violent. Its relentless weight seemed to press on him with choking power. He tried to calm his beating chest. Glancing side to side, he realized that his companions were not visible. Panic began to rise in the pit of his stomach.

"Truss. Ruth. Are you there?" he called out. He reached out around him, hoping to find someone. He groped in the orange glowing smoke. The heat was unbearable, the smoke was offensive to all his senses, and he was terrified.

As he moved through the oppressive darkness, he began to notice eerie sounds that lingered on the air. At first he thought the noise could be the whine of ancient rusty machinery. He stood still to listen more closely. As the sounds grew he could tell that it was not mechanical in nature. The sounds played strangely in his ears as the heat and smoke morphed and strangled them.

"Where are you?" came a slithering, wispy voice. Oscar tensed immediately. He knew that the inhabitants of this realm were dangerous. He did not know if he should run or prepare to fight. He tried to squint through the smoke. Another deeper voice came through the haze. This one sounded like it was behind him.

"Come out, we want to play," said a raspy voice. The laughter that followed filled Oscar with a violent shiver. He clinched his fists, preparing to do- he didn't know what. In front of him, a column of smoke drifted aside long enough for him to get a glimpse of something he hadn't wanted to see.

For a split second, a figure, roughly the size of a man, was revealed through the drifting soot. Beady, narrow eyes stared back at him from a face that looked to be rotting. The flesh hung loose around the stranger's bones. Oscar clenched his muscles tight as the smoke changed directions and hid him again.

The man-like creature had looked directly at him. Oscar wasn't sure what to do. He was certain he wouldn't last long without his star-born companions. *Where had they gone,* he wondered. This was not supposed to be a solo mission. He needed his friends.

"I see you now," came one of the voices through the smoke. Oscar decided to respond with as much strength as he could.

"I come in the name of the Creator King," Oscar said sternly. The smoke and heat made his words dance oddly on the air. "I require passage to—" He was going to say more, but one of the voices cut him off.

"We have no King. We are the uncreated ones," a voice said through the smoke. At the words, a chorus of other voices repeated the statement. Oscar could tell from the cacophony of noise that he was not visited by only two, but by a host of others. There had to be hundreds.

Oscar decided it was time to make a run for it. However, he was not sure where to go. He braced himself to sprint. His muscles tightened as he prepared to bolt. His foot dug into the glowing embers that made up the ground, but before he was able to take a step, something struck.

With impressive force, a body slammed into him from behind. He glanced down as rotting pale arms wrapped around his chest from behind. Without control, Oscar was falling toward the ground. His face buried itself in the smoking ash and embers. He struggled like he never had before.

With explosive power, he shoved away from the burning ground as they flew up into the air. He reached around behind his back and gripped the rotting assailant. Oscar pulled as he let out a guttural growl. The decaying mass of flesh flopped against the ground with a thud. Oscar righted his trajectory so that he would land on his feet.

His landing kicked up simmering coals. He watched his attacker as the bones and drooping flesh of the creature began to turn. The stranger's head spun around in an unnatural way as the mouth spat vile words.

"You're going to be sorry you did that." As the monstrous figure began to rise to his feet, Oscar could hear the crunch of other feet approaching. He looked around quickly, not wanting to be distracted from his attacker. Through the billowing smoke, he saw others, many others, lumbering toward him. His instinct to fight was strong.

Almost without realizing what he was doing, he reached around and grasped the rotting man who had attacked him. By the ankle, Oscar gripped the man-like creature as if he were a weapon. With all his might, Oscar began to swing the zombified man around over his head. The others were close now.

"Stop!" came the voice of the creature who was now being wielded like a medieval mace.

Emerging from the smoke, they came. Other beastly men with rotting flesh and sucked eyes stepped out ready for battle. The orange glow lit their skin in an eerie oscillating light.

Within a fraction of a second, two more were running at him. Oscar spun and dipped to one side. Using his man-mace, he smashed the first enemy. The blow shook the weaponized body that he was holding. The attacker flew back and landed hard in the ash. Oscar used the momentum to strike the other with a powerful blow. He also flipped away with the force.

Oscar spun at the sound of another advance. This time, three blood-thirsty smoke walkers were charging. Oscar's weapon let out a moan as he cracked him like a whip. He rolled and lashed out at one of the assailants. His attempt landed solidly. He kicked out with his foot to best the other. Both flew back, but the third enemy was too quick.

Once more, Oscar felt the rotten arms wrap around him, this time from the front. He let go of the one he had used for a weapon as he tried to pry the monster off. He felt what few teeth his attacker had sink into his neck. Over and over, his enemy bit and squeezed.

Soon, the pressure grew more intense, as another and then another climbed on. The pile toppled to the ground. Oscar tried to fight, but more were joining the fray. He could feel the simmering burn of the coal-covered ground burning his skin. The pile of man-beasts clawed and ripped at him. He shouted out in desperation.

"My King, help me!"

With the crack of bones and the crunch of teeth, the pile began to be peeled back. One by one, Oscar could feel the weight of the mountain of monsters decreasing. He heard screeches and moans as the beasts were thrown from the fray. Within a few seconds, the last enemy was pulled from him.

He looked up to see Truss standing over him. The mighty man reached out to lift Oscar. Once on his feet, Oscar realized that not only Truss but Ruth as well, stood guard. Oscar was tattered and punctures were all over his body. He surveyed the damage quickly but then turned his attention to his two friends.

"Praise the King, I'm glad to see you two," Oscar said.

"Glad you're OK," Truss responded with a slap to his back. Ruth was more serious as they watched the smoke for more attackers.

"What happened?" Oscar asked.

"A tesseract is unpredictable; we all landed in different places. We need to find Zath and his soldiers, or we won't last long." Truss was going to say more, but Ruth cut him off. Her attention was facing out toward the smoky scene.

"More are coming." She looked back. "Many more."

Oscar tensed his muscles again, preparing for another onslaught. He felt the courage rising in his chest, knowing that he would not stand alone this time. He had never been in a celestial battle, but these two seemed to know what to do. He fell in line with them and got ready. Truss whispered to him as the screeches of their enemies grew through the hot air.

"The greatest danger is not physical but mental. No matter what, keep the image of the King in your mind. Let nothing but him dominate your thoughts. When they have subdued us physically the real battle of spirit will begin. Just do your best."

With that, Truss turned and stood next to Ruth. The sound of many grew to a fever pitch of noise pollution. Screeches rose all around them. It had to be hundreds, maybe more. The seconds that followed were the longest of Oscar's existence. He prayed to the King as he tensed his body in preparation.

The enemy hit them like a tidal wave. Hundreds of putrified man-shaped monsters poured in around them.

Oscar swung his fists with as much force as he was able. Staying on his feet was difficult. Out of the corner of his eye, he noticed what Truss and Ruth were doing.

They moved like lightning. Oscar had not ever seen anything like it. Rather than using fist, elbow, or foot they used their entire bodies as if they were the twin hammers of God. Truss moved from foe to foe like a mighty blast. He would leap, tucking his body into a tight ball as he struck each enemy. Landing on his feet, he would repeat the process. He was frightening to watch.

Ruth's approach was somewhat different, although equally as effective. She spun like a tornado with her arms and one leg outstretched. With every revolution, she would twist and bend her body to strike whoever was nearby. She cut through the crowd of monsters like a holy power tool.

Oscar was a novice but it made him feel proud to fight next to these two powerful warriors. Oscar reached for one of the strewn bodies that lay in the embers. As he had before, he used the man-beast as a bludgeon. He tried to stay close to Truss and Ruth, knowing that they were doing ten times as much damage as he was.

The battle went on like this for a few minutes. He was beginning to feel like it was not a lost cause. With these two knowledgeable fighters at his side, there was hope for their survival. He didn't know how many more they would have to fight off, but for the moment, a thin line of positivity was starting to shine through.

After they had battled the rotting horde for a few minutes, there was a break in the fighting. The crowd of enemies had thinned out. Hopefully, their enemies would retreat and give up on the fight. Oscar tossed the body he had been using as a mace. The beast screeched as it soared away, flailing.

Another moment passed before Oscar realized that there was no one else to strike. Truss and Ruth both stood on watch, waiting for more action. Oscar did the same, knowing that the battle was probably not over.

"Summon the Star-born," a slimy-sounding voice called through the smoke. The scene was silent for a long moment as they waited for something to happen. The silence was creepy but not nearly as frightening as what would emerge from the billowing smoke.

The crunch of large feet sounded out from somewhere behind them. They all turned in the direction of the sound.

"This is not good," Ruth said as a giant materialized out of the smoke. Standing at least twice the height of Oscar was a massive juggernaut. The star-born warrior looked like a moving statue of tarnished bronze. Soot and ash swirled around him as he stood motionless in front of them.

His skin was covered in blackish filth, but even the layer of black could not hide the perfect physical form of this fallen star-born celestial warrior. Oscar glanced at Truss and Ruth, not knowing what to do. Star-born warriors were frightening, even when they were loyal to the King. To think that this one was evil filled Oscar with a strange kind of despair. He was fairly certain he was looking at the agent of his own destruction.

He watched as Truss and Ruth clasped their hands together. He had never seen it done before but he had heard stories of warriors who produced starfire. They pressed in tightly as something between their palms began to grow brighter and brighter. His eyes glowed with the sight as Truss and Ruth ignited miniature stars between their hands. They pulled their clasped hands apart to reveal a white hot nuclear ember. Truss produced his first.

Truss pushed with great force as his flaming blade stretched out from his hands. The blade was thick and bright. Oscar marveled at the skill, wishing he had a Starfire sword as well. Ruth's blade followed quickly behind. In short order, she too had a blade of fusion fire. Truss's glowed more blue than Ruth's. Once the blades were stable, Oscar's two companions raised them above their heads and prepared for battle with the fallen star-born warrior.

Oscar had to admire their courage. Battle with a star-born celestial was certainly hopeless, although there was no other option. They had to fight. Oscar wished for Starfire, but as Truss had told him, he would do his best. He clinched his fists and turned toward the star-born giant.

A crowd of dark, rotting figures was circling around the star-born. The zombified audience jeered and screeched like wild animals as they salivated for blood. The screams grew louder by the second.

"We are here to do the will of the King. You must allow us passage," Truss shouted. The voice of the star-born warrior came out like the crunch of steel.

"I am Jothon. I must allow nothing. I have no King, I am the uncreated." With his statement, the crowd of man-beasts erupted. They cheered as if the battle was already won. They repeated Jothon's words in shouting blasts. Oscar glanced at Truss and Ruth to see what they would do. Their starfire blazed hot above their heads. Jothon then added, "You should not have come."

It happened so fast that it took Oscar a second to even realize what had happened. He heard a mighty crunch right next to him first. He then realized that Jothon was no longer standing in front of them. Looking to his right, Oscar realized that where Truss had stood was now Jothon's foot. In the blink of an eye, Jothon had captured Truss between his foot and the smoldering ground.

Ruth reacted like lightning and swung, but it was no use. Jothon reached out for her as if he were catching a fly. Her starfire blade extinguished almost immediately. Oscar faintly noticed that the putrified audience was screeching with delight.

Oscar saw the only opening he would get. With Jothon's attention temporarily on Ruth, Oscar thrust himself forward with all his might. He tucked his body as he had seen Truss do. At his top speed, he slammed into the war giant. It was like hitting a wall of steel.

On impact, Oscar saw a great blast of white. The concussion felt as if it compressed his brain to the size of a grape. He lost consciousness for a split second.

As his mind rebooted, he became vaguely aware that he was being crushed. Something had wrapped itself around him and threatened to turn his body into soup. He felt his bones begin to give. He cried out in pain, something he had not felt in a long time. The jeers of the crowd grew louder still as Jothon made his final move.

With something like the blast of wind, the entire scene changed. Suddenly, Jothon was surrounded by Zath and his six star-born warriors. Their golden skin shone even in this dim, filthy place. Oscar was overjoyed to see the final members of their party arrive.

Zath and his warriors took hold of Jothon. Each of their powerful hands clamped down on the filth-covered war giant with impossible force. Jothon immediately released Oscar and Ruth. He stepped backward, trying to release himself from Zath and his soldiers.

Ruth and Oscar scrambled to pull Truss out of the ash and embers from where Jothon's foot had stamped him down. Truss sat up, still dazed from the smashing. All three watched Zath and his golden celestials struggling against this force of darkness.

It was almost impossible to watch. It happened so quickly that there was nearly nothing to see. Jothon's skin began to burn around the places where Zath's hands touched him. Shortly after, his sooty skin blazed where all the shining warriors held him. In seconds, their incendiary enemy flared like a blazing furnace. Zath spoke the words that made the hair on Oscar's neck stand on end.

"Jothon, the King rebukes you. You shall never again escape the blaze." With that, the glow died down with a flash. Oscar had to blink to understand what he just saw. Only Zath remained. The six other warriors who had subdued Jothon were gone, as was Jothon himself.

Zath turned toward the crowd of rotting, putrified man-beasts and invited them to attack. He scanned over the amassed army of the corrupted dead. They stood their ground, but none dared make a move. Zath raised his voice as his skin glowed brighter.

"Disperse, or be bound," Zath said. A second passed before anything happened. As if it took a moment to sink in, the crowd of dark ones turned and ran. The crunch of hundreds of feet charging away was a strange symphony. Zath stood watch as Oscar turned to Truss and Ruth. Truss was still lying on the ground, shaking from his encounter. Ruth inspected Truss as Oscar spoke to her.

"What was that all about?" Oscar asked. Ruth answered while still feeling Truss's body for fractures.

"They have dragged Jothon off to be bound in a star. There should not be star-born loose among the dead."

"What will happen to Zath's soldiers?" Oscar asked.

"They will return to us when that darkened one is trapped in the blaze once more."

Zath's steps shook the ground as he approached the place where Truss was still sitting. Without a word, Zath stood over them waiting. He stood watch like an ancient stoic statue. Ruth turned to Truss and spoke softly.

"Are you able to stand?" Ruth's voice was little more than a whisper. Truss tried to move but winced in pain. He slumped back down to the ground. His back was smoking from where his clothes touched the hot coals.

"I think everything is broken," Truss said, barely able to speak. His body, like all Elvangaleen, was immortal and incorruptible. He would heal, but it would take time. "In my pocket," he added.

Ruth pulled the flap of his jacket back and reached into his pocket. She pulled from it his leather-bound book. Oscar couldn't understand why he needed his book at that very moment. It didn't seem like he could even move his hands.

"Last page," Truss whispered.

Ruth thumbed through the pages quickly. A clear look of concern and confusion played across her face. She came to the last page. Oscar could not see what she was seeing because of the angle of the book, but he could see her eyes light up.

She reached to the page of the book and pulled from it, something green. In the low light it took Oscar a second to understand what he was looking at. She held it up in front of her face. She looked surprised. Oscar gasped with relief when he realized what it was.

It was a piece of a leaf from the Great Tree in the Holy City. Ruth went to work immediately. She tore a small piece from the leaf and put the rest back in the page of his book. She stashed the book back in his front jacket pocket. She rolled the leaf into a small cylinder.

Knowing what to do, Truss opened his mouth. She placed the leaf on his tongue. He chewed and swallowed. The magic of the leaf took hold quickly. Oscar watched the shape of Truss's body change before his eyes. The leaves of the tree were for the healing of the mortals, but would take effect on anyone who ate them.

Within a few seconds, Truss was beginning to move and test out his limbs. The leaf had played its role. Another few seconds and Truss was sitting up. Ruth helped him to his feet as Oscar watched. He was proud of this resilient and ingenious team.

"We are vulnerable here without my soldiers. We must be on our way," Zath said. He turned and began to walk. The other three followed him. Truss leaned on Ruth and Oscar as he limped along. The leaf had greatly sped his healing, but it would still take time for him to regain his full physical capabilities.

They followed Zath into the heart of Hell.

VALLEY OF PAIRS

By morning, the vines had loosened enough for Abriel to begin to crawl out of the twisted trap. He was ecstatic to be able to move. He paid no attention to the tightness in his neck and back. He wriggled and twisted until his upper body was out of the web of wire-like growth.

He kicked his feet and pushed off of the last branch that held him in place. Finally, he was untethered. He let out an unfettered yell of joy as he lay facing the sky on the forest floor. He could hardly believe that he was no longer trapped. He shouted with excitement once more as he rose to his feet.

Judging by the light that was climbing slowly into the sky, it was early morning. He breathed in the crisp air as if he had woken from a tremendous sleep. He was so thrilled to be alive. He spun around with his arms outstretched as he looked up into the canopy overhead. He remembered his guide with a jolt.

"Thunder, where are you, you handsome little critter?" he said. His exuberance built as he searched the nearby ground for his miniature friend. About five paces away, sleeping at the base of a tree was Thunderfoot. All his appendages were retracted into his shell.

Knowing that it would earn him a bite on the finger or palm, Abriel stepped toward the sleeping shell and picked him up. Thunder opened up and popped his head out immediately. Abriel spun around again with his arms out. He lifted Thunderfoot to his mouth and kissed him on his tiny head. His freedom was too good a thing not to celebrate.

Abriel expected the turtle to bite his hand, but to his surprise, the bite never came. Abriel continued the celebration for another few seconds before he slowed. As his revelry began to die down, Abriel looked to the turtle. He had total faith in him now. Abriel wished he could just speak to the little green guide, but he could see a kind of beauty in the relationship that was forming.

"So what do we do now?" Abriel said to Thunderfoot, who was resting quietly in his palm. He watched closely. The turtle looked back into his eyes for a long moment. He was convinced that his guide was able to communicate, so he waited for instructions.

Thunderfoot lowered his head to Abriel's palm and stuck out his little grey tongue. With a deliberate gesture, the turtle licked the skin of Abriel's hand. The single lick had been so light that if Abriel had not been watching, he would have missed it. He knew that it must mean something.

A rush of warmth washed over the boy. He had not experienced any emotion quite like it. He felt a tickle at the corner of his eye, so he reached up with his free hand. Touching the place, he realized that there was water running down his cheek. He wasn't sure what it meant, but he knew he liked the feeling.

The only relationships he had ever experienced were automatic; this one with his strange little companion was not. It had grown from a seed and was now becoming something special. He could see a strange paradox in the friendship with Thunderfoot. Because it had not come easy, it was more valuable. He knew that it was something he could lose, which made it much more important to cultivate.

He wiped his eye where a second tear was forming. He was so alive with feelings that he could hardly contain himself. He felt like spinning around once more, but decided that it would be better to stay focused. He spoke to his friend in a soft voice.

"Will you let me carry you?" Abriel asked. To his extreme satisfaction, Thunder lowered his head and licked his palm once more. He was thrilled to finally be communicating successfully. Rather than stubbornly head off in a direction of his own choice as he had done before, Abriel patiently asked for guidance.

"Which way do we go?"

Thunderfoot pushed his feet a little farther out from his shell and rose. In Abriel's palm, he turned his little body a few degrees to the east and pointed with his head. Abriel glanced in the direction that Thunder had indicated. It looked as good as any.

Slowly at first, Abriel began walking. He was cautious to avoid being intertwined in a mess of branches and leaves. He could see the value in moving more slowly. Abriel held Thunder out in front of his body like a direction finder. Every so often, Thunder would shift his position in Abriel's hand, letting him know which way to turn. Abriel was truly impressed with his little friend.

Thunder led the expedition like this for the better part of the day. They would periodically stop to eat from the bounty that the forest offered. Their pace was greater than Thunder's would have been on his own, but less than Abriel's would have been by himself. Abriel found the leisurely speed pleasant.

Thunder guided him around all kinds of obstacles, thickets, and obstructions. It felt as if the adventure had finally begun. He enjoyed the scenery as the forest trees began to thin out. The jungled plant life gave way to tall patches of weedy plants with big seedy tops. Long fibrous tendrils stretched from spouts of all colors. They pushed forward until they were completely beyond the forest. The transition had been so gradual that Abriel hardly noticed the change. As the trees became less frequent, Abriel noticed how the tall grasses danced in the wind.

The terrain began to incline as they left the trees behind. Thunder turned in Abriel's hand, pointing them directly toward the peak of a wheat-covered hill. Abriel looked behind to see the forest line stretching out in either direction as far as was visible. The dancing grass tickled Abriel's chest and arms as they made their way up the hill.

The daylight was dipping to an evening amber, and the breeze floated effortlessly by. Abriel breathed in the sweet scent with delight. He played the day over in his mind. It had been a good one. He hoped to have more like it. He felt the smooth tongue of Thunderfoot graze his hand.

"What's the word, Thunder?" Abriel asked playfully. Thunderfoot pulled his legs and tail into his shell. Abriel could feel the cool flat surface of his belly shell against his palm. A few more steps, and Abriel reached the top of the grassy hill. His eyes stayed on Thunder as he came to a halt.

"Are we stopping here?" Abriel asked. Thunder licked his hand as he had before. "That's good, my legs are ready for a rest." Abriel knelt down and placed Thunder in the grass. He stood up to stretch and then lay down for the evening. As he did, he caught his first sight of the valley ahead.

Looking down from the grass-covered hill made his breath catch in his throat. He had never seen anything so wonderful. A pasture stretched out before him for at least the distance of a day's walk, maybe more. The wheat bowed to the wind as it passed along its way. The light from the great city glinted majestically on the tops of a million stalks of grain as they danced side to side.

Although the landscape was magical enough, what captured his imagination was the animals. He watched as countless beasts of all shapes and sizes played, ate, and mingled in the valley below. Birds dotted the sky like black darting stars. Large four legged creatures, the likes of which he had never seen, roamed among the grass, munching slowly. Younglings played in the dusk light.

Abriel was enamored with the valley of life that spread out in front of him. He studied a pair of long necks that swooped their heads down low to bite off mouthfuls of grass. They lumbered slow and deliberate. A pair of four-legged creatures darted by the long necks and grabbed his attention. Their movement was more like bouncing than anything else. Each of their strides was five to ten of Abriel's.

As he let his eyes scan over the lively pasture, he began to notice a kind of pattern. There were at least two of everything. Most pairs looked very similar, but there were slight differences between the two individuals of each pair. He watched a pair of fur covered creatures, noting the differences of each. One of the two was large and powerful, almost a head taller than the other. He would dig and root his nose into the dirt, while his partner would watch. His partner was slightly smaller and shaped subtly different.

He noticed the same kind of interplay between all the creatures below. In all of the pairs the two were never quite identical. Instead they were something more like complimentary. Each worked together seamlessly, while performing different tasks. There was a kind of symmetry to the arrangement of couples.

Abriel wondered why he himself was not in a similar pair. He glanced down at Thunderfoot, who was scratching the ground, trying to unearth something tasty. Abriel could not deny that there was a relationship between himself and his little guide, but it didn't look like the pairing he saw in the valley ahead.

He felt a strange feeling of desire as he let his eyes drift back over the pasture of creatures. He imagined being paired with one of his brothers from the garden. He tried to envision himself in the valley with Eduk, Shameless, or Isod. There was something not quite right about the image. He could not put his finger on the missing piece. There was a mystery in it.

He let the idea roll over in his mind as he knelt down to find a place to rest for the night. He flattened a patch of grass as he wondered about what he had seen. *Why am I not part of a pair?* He thought as he lay his head down. He tried to imagine a partner who was like himself while being different. Something deep inside reached for the image, but it was too difficult to grasp.

He released the vision as his body relaxed into sleep. The cool night breeze played soft as the soundscape of cheerful animals found their places for the night. He slept sound as the world turned beneath him.

THE STARRY LAKE

OSCAR'S EVERY STEP CRUNCHED as it sent cinders into the air. He followed the rest of the expedition party as they walked cautiously across the surface of this alien world of fire. Howls and screams could be heard all around them from the corrupted inhabitants of the place, but with Zath present, they all kept their distance.

"How far must we walk?" Oscar asked. The choking smoke that swirled wildly around them made his voice sound distant and twisted. He expected Truss or Ruth to respond so he was surprised when the usually quiet Zath answered.

"We shall traverse the field of ash until we reach the precipice."

"Oh, I see," Oscar responded, although the explanation only created more questions. He decided to keep them to himself.

If star-born celestials were not such mysterious creatures, Oscar would have been startled at what happened
next. He however decided it was just the way of things.
One by one Zath's companion warriors appeared and fell
in behind their leader. Their shining bodies materialized
and joined the ranks as if nothing had happened.

No doubt, Zath knew that they had returned, but he
gave no greeting or indication that anything had changed.
Oscar silently watched the golden giants from behind
as they walked. *How strange their existence must be,* he
thought. Within a few seconds, all six of the star-born
warriors had returned. They walked in an arc formation,
taking up position around Oscar and the other two. Their
steps fell in perfect unison as they marched through the
desolate landscape.

"We are getting close," Truss said. He pointed out past
Zath at the horizon. Oscar had not noticed before through
the smoke, but the sky ahead was growing bright with orange light. The haze of soot in the air was illuminated with
an eerie glow. With each step, the heat increased. He could
never have imagined such an undesirable environment,
but he guessed that what was over the next hill would be
even worse.

The terrain shifted upward, so they climbed. Now,
sharp spikes of glowing stone jutted up from the ground.

Through cracks in the surface, bright flowing magma angrily churned beneath. Violent lava-born embers fired up from the fissures. Oscar did his best not to step on a crack, as the ancient child's song played comically through his head.

Oscar stared down into the deep rifts in the surface of the world as they passed. His distraction caused him not to notice that the others had stopped their forward progress. Oscar bumped into Ruth's back where she stood. The startle made him stand back and take note of his companions.

"Excuse me, miss," he said to Ruth. Although the apology was not needed, it was an antique habit that he had never broken. Ruth giggled as she responded.

"Even in Hell, you're still a gentleman."

Oscar registered that she had spoken, but his attention was pulled away abruptly. He now saw why the party had stopped. He looked out from the precipice, as Zath had called it. The vision that met him twisted his stomach into a tight knot.

They had stopped at a high place that dropped off in a sheer cliff. Standing at the edge of the crag, Oscar could see out into a massive sea of illumination. Below them stretched out what could only be described as an enormous ocean of glowing white light. It was like looking into the surface of a million burning suns spread over a million light-years of glowing incandescent space. It was a lake of burning plasma for as far as he could see.

He squinted his eyes, trying to see more clearly. As he surveyed the lake of fire below, he realized that it was not a single continuous ocean of flame, but instead a massive cloud of bright burning points. It was an array of countless stars suspended so close to each other that it was almost impossible to tell where one ended and the next began.

There must be some gravitational matrix that holds each star from the next, he thought. In common space, each star would collide with its neighbor. Here every star burned independent of the next as a singular island. The vast lake of fiery stars held a certain kind of beauty in its own way, but Oscar sensed that something sinister was at play. He had heard the name, Lake of Fire, before, but he never guessed that it was something so real. He had always imagined it distant and magical, thinking the name was only an allegory for something less frightening.

"I don't understand," he said, not knowing what else to say.

"The Lake of Fire is the prison for all star-born celestials who rebel against the King. Each point of light is a single celestial imprisoned within a star. These celestials are bound within the heart of the stars and will never escape," Truss said.

Oscar could do nothing but stare down at the burning sea. Even this place where so much evil was trapped still held a beauty that was indescribable. What it represented was a terrible gut-wrenching thing, but the vision that stretched out before him was hard to take his eyes away from.

"It's so-" Oscar began to say, but then could not bring himself to speak the word.

"Beautiful, right?" Ruth asked. "I thought the same thing when I first saw it. I expected it to be awful."

"All things done by the King are beautiful. Even these rebels who intended to thwart his plan have become a part of the divine," Truss said as if it were a somber song.

"So, how do we get down there?" Oscar asked. He was truly afraid to venture any closer to the Lake of Fire. He, however, trusted that the King's plan was good.

"To be among the stars, a star we must be," Zath said. As if the statement were a trigger, the other six star-born giants took up places around Truss, Oscar, and Ruth. Each of the golden warriors reached out and took the hand of the one beside him. The seven celestials began to glow. As the light swelled, a metal ring filled the air. It was slow at first, but grew in intensity until Oscar could see nothing but the seven. After a moment, the figures of Zath and his companions were indistinguishable from each other. They formed one impossibly bright ring of white fiery plasma around them.

The ring began to expand into a sphere in every direction. It slowly closed in above their heads like a bubble of air in a sea of fire. Oscar could feel the ground beneath his feet shaking. The sphere bore into the rock below where they stood. The stone surface began to melt and return to its magma form underneath them. Truss and Ruth joined hands with Oscar as the floor of their star chamber melted away. As the ground became molten lava and flowed out of the mini star, Oscar and his two friends were suspended.

"How exciting," Ruth said with a giggle. "This is the only way to travel."

Oscar caught the joke, but was too frightened to laugh. How were Truss and Ruth so casual in a time like this? He wondered what adventures they must have been on, that this was a time for levity.

They began to accelerate. At first, he could see nothing but the all-encompassing glow of the fission star around them. The inertia of acceleration pressed against his body. Little by little, his eyes adjusted to the impossible brightness. Like a glowing looking glass, he watched the sea of fire rocket by below them at a frightening rate.

They had left the precipice behind with blurring speed. Zath's burning star roared forward like a meteor. Oscar watched the Lake of Fire roar by. Ruth was right, it was an incredible way to travel.

RIDE

ABRIEL WAS FEELING QUITE good. He and Thunder had gotten an early start. The morning beams of light gushed down deliciously on the glade as Abriel and his green guide descended the hill they had spent the night on. He carried Thunder on his shoulder as they spent the morning walking through the valley he had seen the evening before. The animals there were friendly and curious.

Abriel walked slowly, soaking up the morning rays that beamed down. He moved aimlessly through the grass with his arms outstretched. The tall stalks tickled his skin in the most delightful way. The valley was full of the smells and sounds of life.

"It's a lovely morning, isn't it, Thunder?" The turtle didn't respond with words, but Abriel felt as if he could almost hear his companion agree. Their relationship had taken a turn for the better ever since Abriel had been freed from the forest snare. How opposite was the feeling he was currently experiencing.

As he walked in the waisthigh grass a huge Four-Legs came near. It was cautious at first, but when Abriel stopped and stretched out his hand, the beast approached with more courage. It sniffed the air between them with loud flaring nostrils. Abriel could feel the warm blasts of breath that returned from the creature's nose. The enormous animal slowly approached.

When he was close enough, Abriel patted the beast on the side as they got acquainted. The large animal had muscles packed along every one of its sleek lines. Its legs were almost as thick as Abriel's waist, and its head was the size of Abriel's body. As most every animal in the valley did, this huge four-legged creature had a partner, but it kept its distance.

"It's nice to meet you, Friend," Abriel said to the four-legged creature. He then added, "My name is Abriel."

The massive animal turned its head and let out a snort. It was intoxicating to be so close to such a great beast. As Abriel ran his hands over the creature's long fur, he thought about what his teacher had told him.

"You need a name," Abriel said almost without thinking. He let his hand drop as he stepped back from the four-legged behemoth. The spark of creativity began to swell inside his mind. The euphoria of giving such a great creature a name gave Abriel a thrill that was unmatched by any other activity he had yet taken part in. He let his eyes roam over the beast, trying to come up with a suitable title.

As Abriel stepped back, the other of its kind, the partner of the four legs, stepped nearer and took its place beside the first. Now these two quadrupeds stood ready to be named. As if it were a ceremony of the greatest order, Abriel spoke in a loud voice that carried over the valley. His body crackled with excitement as he released the new title into the air.

"All of your kind will be called by the title Trompsteeds." Just as there were twelve other boys back in the garden, Abriel reasoned that there must be other trompsteeds somewhere in Newearth. He was proud to have given the title to such a powerful animal. Although the title was perfect, he felt as if he were not finished.

Somehow, it didn't feel like enough to simply give a title. These two creatures were too gorgeous not to have personal names. Abriel walked around the two trompsteeds as he surveyed their every contour. He noticed certain anatomical differences in the two creatures that he could not quite understand. The one that had first greeted him was the more powerful of the two. However, the one that had come up more timidly was somehow sleeker. There was something subtle that Abriel did not quite comprehend.

He stepped closer and placed his hand on the more powerful of the two trompsteeds. He stroked the fur as he thought about what name might fit such a gorgeous specimen. After a moment of contemplation, he said definitively, "You will be called Myark. Your name will represent strength and power." He then turned to the second of the trompsteeds. Somehow, he knew a name with hard edges was not right. He needed something softer, more elegant. He ventured a cautious hand toward Myark's partner. It let him stroke its fur as Myark had. Softer now, Abriel said more melodically, "You will be called Estra. Your name stands for all that is lovely."

It was as if the trompsteeds could be named nothing else. They seemed to fit their names as well as their own fur fit them. Abriel stepped back, still dazed by the frenzy of excitement that naming these creatures had brought. Myark and Estra stood still as if there was more. Abriel didn't know what to do next. The place had become a magical one. He did not want to leave, but he had a mission to complete.

After a long while, Abriel began to move toward the path that they had been on. He wasn't sure how to communicate to these two creatures that he must be on his way, so he simply took a first step. When he did, Myark snorted loudly. Abriel stopped waiting to understand the trompsteed's action.

With frightening power, Myark raised up on his hind legs and let out a mighty whinny. The ground seemed to shake when his front legs came back down. Abriel expected him to charge away, but that's not what happened. To Abriel's surprise, Myark dropped down to a kneeling position and lowered his head. The unequaled trompsteed was bowing down to Abriel.

"What are you doing?" Abriel asked. As soon as he said it, Estra did the same. Abriel was stunned. He glanced at Thunderfoot, who was still sitting on his shoulder. The turtle offered no advice. Abriel turned back to the trompsteeds as he walked forward. The two bowed beasts made an impressive sight. Standing next to Myark, Abriel reached out once more to stroke the animal's fur. As he did, Myark bounced his head.

Abriel was close enough to feel the trompsteed's breath. He followed the sleek lines of the steed with his hands. His instinct told him that the animal was not just bowing, but offering his service. Cautiously, Abriel placed himself next to Myark and gripped his mane. With an unpracticed grace, Abriel swung his right leg over the trompsteed's back.

As soon as the boy was on Myark's back, the great four-legged giant rose to his full height. Abriel let out a gasp, not knowing what to expect. He watched as Estra, Myark's companion, also raised up. They both let out a mighty neigh as if they were speaking to each other. Myark stomped the ground below with a powerful thrust. Abriel could feel Myark's muscles jolt beneath him.

Without warning, Myark and Estra broke into a run. Abriel squeezed the beast between his knees and gripped the mane even tighter. The grassy valley rocketed by at blurring speed. Abriel had never imagined he could move so fast. The wind soared by as they galloped. With the excitement, Abriel let out a cry of joy.

He felt Thunderfoot slipping from his shoulder. Letting go of the mane with one hand, he reached and grabbed his shelled friend just in time. Thunder retracted into his shell as Abriel devoted one hand to carrying him. The other held the steed's hair as he did his best to move with the rhythm. Abriel let out another shout as the world buzzed by.

The other animals in the valley stopped to stare at the boy on his mount. *Nothing has ever been seen in this world,* Abriel thought. Every step felt like a leap. Each stride was ten, or maybe twenty of Abriel's. He would be to the great mountain in no time, that is, if they were going in the right direction.

Holding on with only one hand meant he was lopsided. Abriel adjusted himself on Myark's back. As he did, the great beast began to shift directions. The trompsteed leaned hard into the turn. Abriel had to do the same to stay on. As he did, he realized with another wave of exhilaration that Myark had responded to his movement. He had thought it enough to gain a ride. He had not dreamt that he would be in control. Once again, he let out a jubilant yell.

"All-right My-ark!" he sang. His voice broke with each jostle of his mount. The sound that came out of his mouth made him laugh, which also sounded strange. He squeezed Myark harder between his knees as he let out another shout. "Le-ts go fa-st-er My-ark!"

With that, the trompsteed ducked his head and poured on the speed. So fast, in fact, that Estra was falling behind. It felt as if they were not touching the ground at all. Creatures from all over the valley let out wild cries of excitement at the sight. Abriel leaned down low in order to hang on. He tried to grip harder with his knees, but he was beginning to be shaken free of his ride. Almost unable to hold on, Abriel shouted.

"N-ot so fa-st." As he did, Myark slowed to a trot. A moment later, Estra had caught up. Abriel was breathing hard, as was his ride. He relaxed a little. His inner thighs were burning with the exertion. His heart was beating as fast as it ever had. Abriel let out another laugh.

"That was great!" He held out the hand that held Thunderfoot. "Are you still in there, Thunder?" Holding the shell up to his face, the turtle peeked his head out for a split second to make sure it was safe. When he was convinced he could come out, he dropped his belly and pushed his legs through the openings. Abriel placed Thunder on Myark's back in front of him.

"Ok, Thunder, which way?" Abriel said. With that, the four of them turned and headed toward the horizon. Abriel was humming with excitement. He could not believe the adventures that the world held. He wondered how he could have ever been trepidatious about leaving the garden. He felt like he had not truly lived until now.

EVENT HORIZON

OSCAR SCANNED THE HORIZON of fire as he and the others rocketed over countless light-years of burning stars. As a plethora of fiery prisons blurred by, Oscar marveled at the sheer number of captured celestial beings. He found it impossible to comprehend the immeasurable scale to which this place of scorching plasma was built.

There were stars of all sizes, some burned small and orange. Others were so large that Oscar could hardly believe they were single suns. Some raged like great blue infernos. Each star represented a rebel child of the King. Each once reflected the glory of the Great One, but now the only light they gave served as a reminder of their impossible treachery.

"There," Truss said, although it was not words that he heard but the intention. He glanced at Truss and found him pointing to the horizon line. Oscar trained his eyes out past the transparent wall of their star sphere and looked for the thing to which Truss was referring. At first, he saw nothing that stood out as unique.

He watched as they careened in the direction he had indicated. As the burning stars blasted by, Oscar thought he could make out a distinction in the array of star fission fire. There seemed to be some kind of change in the distance. The glow that emanated from the sea of fire was incredibly bright, but for some reason, the far horizon seemed dark.

Was it possible that they were getting to the far edge of the Lake of Fire? The massive ocean of blaze seemed as if it could have no end. Oscar had imagined that it went on forever. However, growing in front of them was a blackness. It was not that there was anything to see, but that was exactly the strange thing. It was as if his eyes were unable to see past the edge that they were approaching.

Almost as soon as he realized the dark anomaly, he sensed the unmistakable inertia of deceleration. As they began to slow down, Oscar leaned forward as if it would help him see more clearly. There it was, like a crack in the fabric of space- nothingness. It seemed as if even space itself had fled from it. A dark spot grew, and to Oscar's intense discomfort, they were heading right for it.

"It's the event horizon of the maglo-pit," Ruth said to Oscar as if that meant anything to him. He knew what an event horizon was. He had even seen a few in his lifespan, but this was unlike anything he had ever experienced. It was as if there was nothing there. Even spatial black holes emit small amounts of material. This was like looking into an utter void.

He could hardly stand to stare into the point of nothingness so he let his eyes drift out toward the edges of it. A ring of lesser black encircled the void. Like it, another set of lesser darknesses spilled out in concentric circular patterns from the dark point.

Oscar noticed that all of the other stars now seemed to be in the distance. He looked out beyond the black point and realized that they had not reached the edge of the Lake of Fire. Instead, as far as he could tell, they were in the dead center. In the far distance, there were millions more stars like the ones they had already passed. It was as if all the stars were orbiting around this central black point. The darkened hole in space was at the middle of the ocean of plasma, which itself was an enormous spiral galaxy. At the center of this giant galaxy was the darkest black hole Oscar could possibly imagine.

They came to a stop over the dark center of the burning sea of fire. *Please*, he thought, *don't let this be our destination.* He hoped with everything in him that they were only slowing down to admire the view. Considering there was nothing to see, he realized that was unlikely. Now hovering over the darkest point inside or outside the universe, Oscar could feel its gravity tugging at him. His weight had increased under the gravitational strain. Every atom in his body had increased to ten times its former mass.

"Is that a—" Oscar began to ask, but trailed off.

"It's a maglo class black hole," Truss said, as they all looked downward. The point of black seemed to swallow all the light that the surrounding stars drenched it in. "The Tempter of Twisted Light has escaped a star prison before. So the King encased him at the pitted center of a maglo-class black hole. One has never existed within the universe. It's another reason that this place had to be built outside the created kingdom. It would destroy the fabric of space time if it were housed within."

"Wow," was all Oscar could say. He was stunned. The scene gripped him with fear. He was having trouble understanding why he had been chosen for this mission. He was nothing compared to these types of forces. His emotions stormed inside of him. His guts seemed to twist into knots. He reminded himself to blink as he stared down into the most destructive point that had ever existed.

Oscar gasped as he felt the sensation of falling. It was as if the floor had dropped out of a tall tower. He looked to Ruth and Truss for understanding. They were moving downward with him. He glanced toward his feet and saw that they were falling toward the black hole. He reached out and gripped Truss for assurance. Their eyes met. Somehow, Truss was calm and collected.

"We have to descend to the event horizon. That is where you will give your message to the Tempter," Truss said. Ruth, too, reached out to assure Oscar. When he looked at her, he thought he could see a tinge of fear, but she covered it well.

"I am to give a message?" Oscar asked. "What message? I don't have a message. I was given no message to relay." He was breathing hard now. Ruth squeezed his shoulder as she spoke softly.

"Don't worry, Oscar, the King will give you the words when the time is right."

Oscar could hardly hear her over the noise in his head. They continued to speed as they fell toward the black nothing that lay below. Oscar watched the void of darkness swelling below him as they descended into the heart of Hell. He hoped he would be able to do what he was sent to do.

"My King, steady my fearful heart," Oscar whispered.

RUSH

ABRIEL HAD BEEN RIDING Myark, the powerful tromp-steed, all morning. Myark's loyal companion Estra trotted alongside as they drove forward toward their destination. Thunderfoot had made very few corrections along the way. Abriel was having such a good time that he had thought very little about his mission, but was simply enjoying the adventure.

There were other animals that had trailed along. Everywhere they went the creatures were curious. Some would come out from their hiding holes and follow along for a short time. Some of the more sure footed had been trailing in their wake for hours. It was as if there was an audience to watch the adventure unfold.

Along the way, Abriel had named the animals that joined them from atop his mount. He would bestow names with a loud, formal voice as they rode along. All told, he had named hundreds of animals along the way.

There were creatures that walked on two legs. There were critters that galloped on four. There were even beasts that came down from the sky and perched on Myark or Estra just long enough to receive a name before flying away.

The day so far had been very rewarding. One by one, Abriel was naming and categorizing his world. He had come up with certain rules for how each was named. He had divided them all into categories. When naming, he would consider things like number of appendages, if they had wings, and whether they had fur or smooth skin.

He knew that there was so much to learn about the creatures of Newearth, and he could not wait to discover more about the ones he'd named so far. He called the broad categories "kinds." He noticed that the similarities between most animals allowed them to be grouped into about five different kinds. Right there on the back of Myark, he had spent the morning conceiving an entire naming convention for all of the creatures.

The categories he made for naming worked pretty well, but there were definitely creatures that didn't appear to fit into any group. There was the one he named Egrastra. It had wings which made him think it should be among the Flyers, as he had come to call them. However, it had four hoofed feet which meant that it should be within the Gallopers group.

There were others that baffled him, such as the Ipsontar. It had a beak like the flyers, but its skin was smooth and scaly, much like the Crawlers' kind. Creatures like the Egrastra and the Ipsontar he put in a group of their own that he called Wonderers. Partly because they made him wonder many things about them, and partially because they filled him with awe.

He had been so caught up in the naming of the creatures that he had paid little attention to where Myark and Thunderfoot had taken him. After hours of riding and naming he realized that the creatures who formed the following audience around them all had names. He was sure that more would join as they went along but for now he focused his attention to the trek at hand.

The landscape had changed drastically since the morning. Myark and Estra were able to cover so much more ground than Abriel ever could by himself. He guessed that what they had done in one morning would have taken him at least a few days had he been on foot.

There were more rocks that were strewn about the ground than there had been when they started that morning. The plants that grew there were short and bushy. The terrain was pitching upward and Myark had slowed his pace. With each step loose rocks would shift and move.

The sound of stones had a soothing effect on Abriel as they pressed on.

He looked back at the host of creatures that were following. The rocky terrain was too much for some. In the distance, Abriel could see a trail of creatures that had turned back. Still, animals of all kinds continued to follow like a curious parade of life. Overhead, winged ones circled. Abriel felt honored to be at the head of such an eclectic crew.

As he was looking back, he was startled by the abrupt stop. Myark pawed at the ground. Abriel turned to see what had halted their forward motion. In front of them, a landscape stretched out for as far as he could see. Myark's feet were perched at the edge of a great cliff that overlooked the land below. Abriel had never seen anything so glorious.

The sheer drop off that stood in front of them descended sharply for about a hundred body lengths until it flattened out and stretched forward into the scenery. Abriel stared over the cliff edge and then let his eyes roam out over the view. The valley below had interspersed patches of green but primarily was made up of rocky spires that jutted up from the ground.

As he drank in the dazzling scenery, he noticed something on the far horizon. It did not slope slightly in the familiar curvature but instead spiked up sharply into a great peak. Out there at the edge of the world was a mountain. As he looked, he knew that it was not just any mountain; it was *the* Mountain. It was his mission.

Abriel strained his eyes to gain any information about the faraway place. He guessed that it was another day's walk from the cliff where he now stood. He felt the excitement of a mission coming to completion. "There it is," he whispered to himself. If he hurried, he estimated, he could be there within another day. Keeping his eyes on the distant mountain, he patted Myark to let him know he was climbing down.

Abriel kicked one leg in order to dismount the trompsteed. As he did, Myark bent a knee and allowed him to climb off gently. He grabbed Thunder and put him on his shoulder. He stepped closer to the cliff and peeked his head over the edge. It was nearly straight down, but he thought there were enough places in the rock to grip. He visualized himself climbing down it. He traced a path with his eyes. After a long few moments of contemplation and study, he turned back to the animals that were gathered behind. He wasn't sure if they could understand, but he didn't know how else to communicate.

"I'm going to climb down. Any that are able, are free to join me," he said. The faces of the creatures did not portray understanding. The mass of animals kept their eyes on him, but he was almost sure they didn't have a clue what he was saying. "I guess you will understand when I climb over the edge."

A sharp sting bit into his ear on the side where Thunderfoot was perched. Abriel quickly grabbed the turtle from his shoulder and held him out in front of himself. He rubbed his ear where his guide had bitten him. It had been days since the little green beast had done that.

"Why did you bite me?" Abriel asked. In Abriel's hand, Thunder turned his body to point down the length of the cliff. Abriel had gotten much better at discerning his guide's instructions. Abriel scanned the line of the cliff in the direction that Thunder was pointing. He could see that it sloped downward. He quickly understood what the turtle meant to say. If they followed the ridge line of the cliff, they would eventually meet the valley.

Abriel looked out past the cliff at the Great Mountain. It felt almost close enough to touch, but still so far away. He looked in the direction that Thunder was pointing. It would certainly add time to the trip. Abriel let out a sigh.

"If we go that way, it will take us at least an extra day, maybe two." He watched Thunder, but the little critter didn't move. Thunder was so stubborn. Abriel looked over the edge again, reassuring himself of his ability. "I've climbed trees since I was little. I can climb down this cliff.

If we go this way, we can be at the base of the mountain by tomorrow."

Thunder stood like a statue, pointed toward the ridge line. Abriel knew that Thunder's path was safer, but he wanted to try the cliff wall. *What's the worst that could happen,* Abriel thought. He wasn't sure of the answer to that question. *Surely, Teacher would not have sent me on a task that was too much for me to handle.*

"I will try to climb down, if it is too difficult, we will go your way." Abriel reached out and placed Thunder on Myark's back. He spoke to him more gently as he laid his hand on Thunder's shell. "If I can find a path, I will return to carry you down."

Thunderfoot craned his neck, opened his mouth, and bit Abriel's finger. It stung a little, but Abriel did not jerk his hand away. He knew what his guide was telling him, but he stood his ground.

"I know you disagree, but I plan to try. If it works, it will save us so much time. The quicker we get down from this cliff, the quicker we arrive at the mountain." Thunder reached out to bite him again, but Abriel pulled his hand away before he could. He then added, "I'll be right back."

With that, he stepped toward the edge of the cliff and began to look for the best place to start his descent. After locating a spot with a good outcrop of rocks, he turned around with his back to the drop-off. He glanced at all the creatures who were gathered to watch. He wondered if they had any idea what he was doing.

He laid down on his stomach and began to scoot toward the sheer face feet first. He let his legs dangle over the edge as he searched for the footing he had seen. Another backward lunge and his chest was at the edge of the rock. His heart beat fast. He noticed that his hands were sweating. He tingled as the sensation of fear washed over his body. He had not anticipated what his emotions would do.

He stretched his feet out, trying to gain purchase. His toe touched something solid, so he released his weight from his arms just a little. Now he clung to the rock surface by his fingertips. He turned his head to the side, trying to see anything other than the stone in front of him.

He let go with one arm and reached for another handhold that was a little lower. As he did, he realized that he had made a mistake. The handhold was a mistake. The attempt to descend the cliff was a mistake. Not listening to his guide was a mistake. He wished that he had realized it just a few moments before.

His sweaty fingers slipped from the narrow grip that he had been grasping. His foot then faltered and jerked loose of the crag it had been resting on. In another fraction of a second, he was completely free of the wall and falling through the open air.

His stomach was in his throat. He heard a yell come from his mouth, but he had no control over it. He tumbled upside down once, twice, three times, before something struck him on the left shoulder. It all happened so quickly. He was disoriented. Pain exploded in his shoulder as the trajectory of his body violently changed. Now tumbling the other direction, he shouted out.

"Save me, My King!" He didn't even know what it meant. He had heard Oscar say things about the Great King a number of times. He'd never met the King, nor did he even know anything about him. It just slipped from his lips unsolicited. He had no time to consider the statement as he fell.

Abriel soared downward faster and faster. For a brief moment, he felt that he was motionless. His body was suspended in nothing, as if the sky and the ground fought for him with equal pull. The moment was torn from him with terrible aggression. He was falling with more speed now.

He had no time to react. The stone basin rushed at him like a tidal wave of rock and earth. He put his arms out instinctively, but it did nothing to slow him. A white blast

of light erupted across Abriel's vision as his body crumpled
against the rocks that lay at the base of the cliff.

RELEASE

OSCAR FELT THE CHANGE in inertia as if his guts were being pulled downward with lead weights. The sensation of falling was replaced with intense gravity. It exerted more bodily pressure than anything Oscar had every experienced. He felt the skin on his face being pulled toward the black hole that stood beneath.

"Once we breach the event horizon, we will only have a moment. Zath and the others will not be able to keep us out of the hole for long," Truss said. His voice sounded strained. Oscar looked to he and Ruth. Their faces looked like his felt. Their skin sagged as if it were being drawn downward. Oscar nodded to show that he understood.

The glowing orb that encased them began to vibrate and rumble with violent oscillations. It made Oscar feel a little ill to think that there was only a thin sphere wall that stood between him and annihilation. It was as if Zath and his companions were struggling with all their might to keep from dropping into the pit.

A powerful explosion erupted around Zath's spherical star structure. Oscar assumed they had reached the event horizon. The concussion sent jolts of pain up through Oscar's entire body. He touched his torso to make sure he was still intact. The pain was only instantaneous and passed quickly. There seemed to be no damage done.

The light that came from below them was dim at first, but grew steadily brighter as they descended. Oscar was surprised. He had expected there only to be darkness below the event horizon. The deeper they went and brighter the light grew. It wasn't the warm orange light that many of the stars gave off. It was tinged with tones of violet and blue.

Zath's star bubble emerged on the interior of the event horizon as if it floated to the surface. The aggressive vibration halted immediately. The intense gravitational pull still persisted. It had grown stronger with every inch they moved downward. It felt as if his body would collapse on itself any second.

Now that they had broken through the edge of the black hole event, Oscar could not see anything. It was not by darkness that he was blinded, but by light. It was so impossibly bright that his eyes were not able to adjust. He tried to close them and then cover them with his palms. He could see the bones of his hands as if he were looking into an X-ray sun. No matter what he did, he could not escape the immeasurable light.

It was coming from below his feet. It didn't matter if he turned his head the other direction; the blue scorching light permeated everything. The blazing intensity of the illumination made him feel as if he would break apart or burst into flames.

"Oscar, it is time." He was not sure who had said it. He could see nothing other than the blinding blaze of bluish-white. His body felt as if it were being burned from the inside. Oscar had no idea what he was supposed to say. He hoped that the King would give him the right words. He lowered his head and directed his voice toward the great source of light. Words came from his mouth. It was a strange feeling. It was as if the King was using his voice. The words were not Oscar's.

"Archetype, Awake!" Oscar's voice shouted. The sphere shook with the immense power of his voice. It sent chills up and down Oscar's body. With the words, a violet shock wave blasted out. Impossibly, the searing light grew even brighter, as it took on a more violent heat. In response to the blast, Oscar's voice spoke again.

"Once more, you are invited to tempt the hearts of men. You may attempt to twist the light that is inside them. If you succeed, you may stay free for as long as a rebellious heart remains within the Kingdom. If you fail, you must return to this prison."

A deep silence followed. It was as if the life of the universe could fit in that single moment of quiet. The silence was followed by another blast of violet light. This time, the concussive eruption pulsated with undulating regularity. Oscar felt the pulse, although his eyes were useless in the brightness.

"Do you accept these conditions?" Oscar's voice said. This time, there was no pulse, but something about the light began to change. Oscar could not tell what it was at first. After a moment, he realized that the light was focusing. Although it did not dim in intensity, the source of light was growing more refined. Within a few seconds, the light was no longer permeating everything, but instead shining brightly from one single point.

Oscar looked past his feet to the epicenter of the brilliance. He now saw that what was an enormous orb of unadulterated illumination was now changing in form. He could not decide if it was shrinking or growing larger. He assumed it was one of those upper-dimensional things that made it impossible to understand.

The burning star that was suspended at the center of this black hole was taking definite shape. It contorted and morphed as if it were no star at all. It was like looking into the center of a furnace full of molten gold. The star's edges became more precise. The light was not any more dim than it had been, but it turned inward, instead of blasting out as it had. The light waves were somehow morphed and bent.

The star could no longer be called a star. Although the form was not as well defined as a terrestrial man, it had taken on the shape and form of a person. The body now glowed like a million burning suns, but the light was somehow trapped. This so-called Archetype could twist the light that shone out. He could twist it back to shine on himself. Oscar could hardly understand what he was seeing.

The man-star stayed suspended in space for only a second. Then he was gone. There was no flash of light. There was no jump path. He was just gone. Oscar blinked in the sudden relative darkness. The event horizon had apparently collapsed on itself. He could now see all of the other star prisons that surrounded them. They were bright, but were dim compared to what he had just experienced. He sighed in relief.

"The Tempter of Twisted Light has been released, the Archetype of evil is free," Truss said.

Oscar's relief dissolved. *What have we done,* he thought. He imagined the pain he had just unleashed on the universe. This single event could be the beginning of countless years of rebellion and agony. He remembered the destruction that the Archetype had caused on the previous Earth.

"Let's go home," Ruth said. Oscar nodded, but his mind was somewhere else.

BROKEN

PAIN LIKE ABRIEL HAD never felt coursed through his body. He had experienced the mild abrasions of boyhood play, but this was different. He was immersed in a deep, persistent agony emanating from his right leg. He tried to adjust his body so that it would not hurt as much, but each attempt at moving shot violent blasts through his entire being.

He must have passed out because he remembered losing his grip on the rock wall, but everything after that was fuzzy. He leaned cautiously against a rock at the bottom. There was blood everywhere. He had never seen so much come from a wound so quickly. In fact, he had only ever seen light scratches and cuts, few of which ever revealed the inky red rivers below. The bleeding made him lightheaded. He had left his creature friends at the top of the cliff. There was little they could do, even if they were to find their way down.

It may have been hours, or it may have been minutes, but eventually Abriel was able to calm himself enough to assess the damage. Most of the pain and blood seemed to be coming from his leg. Everything else still hurt from the impact, but not nearly as much as his lower extremity. He wondered if his sense of sight had been knocked out of alignment, because his leg looked bent in a way that it never had before.

Instead of bending only at the knee, the ankle, and the hip, there was a new joint halfway up his thigh. He thought it was no coincidence that this was the same place from which most of the crimson was oozing. This new turn in his leg was most definitely undesirable. The excruciating sensation it offered was one of a kind. He understood very little of the inner workings of his own body, but he reasoned that the structure on which his flesh was built was not indestructible. He had found its limits, and the discovery was one he would like to undiscover.

Abriel had also noticed a strange thing occurring with a certain regularity. Involuntarily a shout would escape his mouth every few moments. He could do nothing to stifle the cry. It was so closely connected with the pain, there seemed nothing to do but let the screams come. So he cried and yelled, wishing he had listened to his guide.

Something passed into his peripheral vision. Abriel glanced up quickly, although he could not stop the cry that was coming from his mouth. The shape of a person stood nearby. This person, however, did not have the simple terrestrial look that Abriel had grown accustomed to. A silhouette was all he could see, but instead of the shape being cast in shadow, it was made of pure light.

Abriel, still conscious of his pain, squinted his eyes to try to understand what he was seeing. Slowly, the figure's radiant form dimmed. It reminded him of the Elvangaleen that had forbidden him to return to the garden. However, this one was somehow different. Abriel watched as the person walked toward him.

As he approached, Abriel saw that the figure was a male, like himself, but he had the look of years, both young and old at the same time. As the man walked toward him, Abriel noticed his face. It was kind and had the appearance of concern and confidence. He was not in a hurry, but he moved deliberately toward where Abriel was lying.

The man knelt down next to Abriel. The glow had gone out of him. He now looked no more alien than the boy. For a long few moments he said nothing. He could feel his heart beating. The pain was still present but it had somehow taken on a secondary role. The man who knelt had Abriel's full attention.

"Who are you?" Abriel asked.

"You know who I Am," the man said. His voice was gentle.

"I do?" Abriel said. The man's eyes shifted to the rocky cliff from which Abriel had fallen and then back down to the boy.

"You called out to me a moment ago," the man said. Abriel glanced at the rock above as if there were some secret locked away in the stone. With sudden clarity, he recalled his words. As he fell, he had shouted out. The man spoke as if he, too, could see the memory in Abriel's mind.

"Save me, My King," the man said, repeating Abriel's words. Wide-eyed, he looked at the man in wonderment. He had heard his teacher speak of the King, but never had he imagined that he would appear so much like a man. In fact, Abriel had never imagined that he would appear at all. The King had been a distant idea, a faraway thought, but here he was.

"You're the King?" Abriel asked.

"It is as you say."

"What is a King?" He said. The man chuckled lightly much like his teacher might. Abriel could see some similarities in the King. Although he suspected that the attributes originated with this man, not with Oscar. The familiarity made Abriel feel warm.

"Through me, everything was made. Without me nothing was made that has been made. In me is life, and that life is the light of the world."

Abriel felt as if he could consider the King's words for days, and still not fully understand what he meant. His words were rich and full of powerful meaning. He spoke as if the words were only thin bark that represented a great, ancient trunk beneath. Abriel wished he could respond more intelligently, but before he could stop it, he was asking another question.

"Are you from the Great City?"

"No, the Great City is from Me," the King said. Abriel twisted his face up in confusion. He tried to rephrase his question, thinking that the wording was wrong.

"I mean, do you live in the Great City?"

"No, The Great City Lives in Me."

"Oh," he paused, not understanding. "So the Great City is alive?"

"In me is life; those who are in me live."

"So those who are not in you are not alive, like rocks?"

"The rocks that are in the kingdom are more alive than those who are not."

Abriel had no idea what that meant. He thought back to his teacher's lesson on paradoxes. He now wished he had paid more attention. The King was full of fascinating and impossibly deep mysteries. Abriel felt as if he could talk to the King forever and never run out of questions to ask. He could see it in his mind. Each answer he got would create ten more questions. The experience was as desirable as any fruit he had ever tasted.

"Now I have a question for you," the King said. "There were two plants that grew in an attractive garden. Their gardener instructed them both to grow fruit that was sweet for eating. The first plant began to grow a single melon. All day, this is all the plant did. The melon grew sweeter by the minute. The second plant, however, began to grow multiple things. First, it grew a stalk that was flavorful. It then grew beans that were good for eating. Finally, when the day was nearly done, it began to grow fruit as the gardener had asked.

The next morning, the gardener arrived to see the fruit his plants had made. He pulled the melon from the first plant and found it to be delicious, for it was all that plant had done all day long, and it was exactly what he had wanted. He then turned to the second plant. He discovered that it had grown edible stalks, beans, and a very small fruit. He said to the plant, "I have other plants with edible stalks. I have other plants with beans that are good for eating. Because you have done tasks I have not given you, the one task I have given you, you have done poorly."

Abriel was astounded. Oscar was a good teacher, but never had he taught like this. The King was a master of imagination. Abriel wondered at the meaning of the story. He was about to ask what it meant when the King continued.

"My question is, Abriel, which plant do you wish to be?"

It took him a moment to understand. When the story clicked into place, Abriel felt like he had fallen from the rock face all over again. A thrill passed through his body only momentarily. There was no shame in it, but Abriel could see himself in the story. He understood that there was a lesser joy to be had. There was a greater faithfulness to be accomplished.

As he considered the King's story he began to unravel the meaning. The first plant was faithful and did exactly as he asked. The second plant was busy with its own tasks. It too was faithful but because it had busied itself with tasks of it own, it was not as faithful. Abriel had never seen the idea of faithfulness so clearly. He longed to be the first plant. He longed to be faithful to the king. Concern filled his mind.

"I wish to be like the first plant, but I fear I am the second?" Abriel said. His world hung on what the King would say. All he wanted in that moment was to please the King. He wished with all his heart to be whatever the King wanted him to be. There was no fear in it, only joy in the knowledge of pleasing him. The King smiled as he responded.

"As of yet, you are neither, for the day is not done."

Abriel could have jumped up and danced with joy. There was still opportunity to please his King. How quickly he had become enamored with this benevolent ruler. He had to know more about him. It was as if his heart was burning inside his chest with every word that the King said.

Abriel knew what he had to do. It was not going to be easy, but he had to get to that mountain. It was his one task. It was his fruit to bear. He looked out past the King to the horizon. He took a deep breath and placed his hands on the rock that he leaned against. The simple motion forced the eruption of a fresh wave of pain. It rippled through his body, leaving nothing untouched. Abriel shouted out in agony, but he was determined.

His muscles shook as he lifted himself up from the rock. The King stood and let Abriel struggle. He didn't wish to dishonor the King by being too weak to stand. His left foot held most of his weight, as his right dangled. It was like a tree branch that broke, whose bark had not fully come apart. His pain level shot up tenfold. Still, he was determined.

Finally, he was up. His lightheadedness turned to nausea, another sensation he had never experienced. Tears ran down his face. He only hoped that the King would know that the tears and the pain were in order to honor him. Abriel could hardly believe how strongly his emotions ran. It was as if he had only been sleeping until this moment. *Do all who meet the King change so much in so little time,* Abriel thought.

He felt as if he were a new person. He had died in the fire of agony, reborn in pain, but he believed in one thing now. He believed in the King. He couldn't explain it. He didn't know exactly what it meant but knew as long as the King was with him he could believe in nothing else so strongly.

The King watched as Abriel put his broken leg out. He tried to put weight on it, but quickly found that it would not hold. It felt like something sharp was clawing at the inside of the flesh. The pain narrowed his vision and made him see little dancing spots around the edges. He wondered if he could stay standing.

He tried a new strategy. Instead of walking he hopped on his one good foot. It jostled his broken leg which made him feel like he might explode. He had moved a single pace toward the mountain. It was going to be a long trip if every step was this painful, but he would accept it if it meant it pleased his King.

The King placed his hand on Abriel's shoulder. He smiled widely as he helped steady the boy. His expression was warm and inviting. Abriel only hoped that it was the smile of satisfaction. He took another wobbly step, but nearly fell with the pain. He was afraid of failure. He was afraid that the excruciation would grow so intense that he would have to stop. As another blast of agony shot through his body, Abriel winced.

"Is it possible for life to end because of great pain?" Abriel asked between gasps.

"In this world, death is not necessary, but it is possible."

Although he had never heard the word *death* before he quickly gathered its meaning. He considered what it would mean to cease to live. He was unsure of what might come after that. His mind raced as he tried to take another step. He wondered if every conversation with the King was filled with such learning. Thoughts that would usually remain unsaid bubbled to the surface almost without his intention. He heard his own voice expressing his inner desire.

"I hope this pain does not bring my death."

"Do you believe in me?" the King asked as he helped him with another step.

"How could anyone not believe?" Abriel asked as he continued to hop.

"There are those who have not believed even though they have seen my face."

Abriel could not understand how that could be possible. He glanced at the face of the King and found so many things. Behind those ancient eyes was wisdom. Beneath the scars on his skin were stories that Abriel longed to know. There was nothing about this King that Abriel could deny.

"Because you believe, I will give *you* life forever," the King said. "And I see that the life I've given you is already bearing fruit." He gestured to Abriel's broken leg.

This filled him with another jolt of exuberance. He was thrilled that the King saw his sacrifice as fruit. He wanted to please him more, so he took another painful step. His leg gave out beneath him, and he began to fall. The King's strong hands steadied him before he could tumble.

"Do you want me to take the pain away?" the King asked with compassion.

"My King, I am afraid that if you take the pain away, I will forget the lesson I have learned here," Abriel said.

"Your's is a rare kind of devotion. I am honored by it. You are learning that to receive things of great value, it is worth enduring great pain."

Abriel had to think about this for a moment. Because each step took all of his concentration, he paused to consider the King's words.

"I can see the truth in it," Abriel said, but then added, "Have you ever felt pain?"

The King reached out his hands and offered them for Abriel to look upon. Abriel ran his fingers across the King's palms. In each, there were small holes that he could see through to the ground. The King explained slowly.

"As you are suffering a little to bear fruit, I had to suffer much to bring this kingdom to bear."

Abriel could not imagine what "suffer much" might mean if what *he* was currently experiencing was "little." He steadied himself and prepared for another step. The King placed his hand on his shoulder as if he intended him to wait another moment.

"To make your burden lighter, your companions are arriving," the King said.

At that very moment, Abriel heard the stomp of galloping. He turned to look in the distance under the shadow of the cliff wall. The sound echoed loudly as Myark, the powerful trompsteed, charged forward. He whinnied loudly when he caught sight of the boy. Abriel could have cried seeing his friend charging in to save him.

Abriel turned to the King, but he was no longer there. He twisted around, with considerable pain, to see where the King had gone, but he had vanished. Abriel turned back to his friend, who galloped right up, breathing heavily. Behind him by quite a bit, unable to keep up with his impossible speed, was Estra, Myark's companion. A bevy of birds that Abriel had not yet noticed circled overhead.

Myark came close and offered his neck for Abriel to steady himself. He accepted thankfully with both hands. He clung to the trompsteed as another wave of pain washed over his body. He laid his head across Myark. Thunderfoot was sitting on Myark's back, quite rattled by the trip. The turtle clung to a strand of the steed's mane with his mouth. He had, no doubt, been tossed about in the gallop, but if there was one thing Thunder had going for him, it was his bite strength.

Abriel patted Myark and nuzzled his nose with Thunder. He was immeasurably glad to see his friends. He had wondered if he would ever lay eyes on them again. His decision to climb down the cliff was poorly planned, but it had earned him a meeting with the King. He could hardly wish to trade that for anything. Estra came up behind Abriel and squeezed him between herself and Myark. It was the closest thing to a hug either of them was able to do.

"I am so glad to see you all," Abriel said with tears in his eyes. He could not distinguish between the pain in his body and the joy of having his friends back. "So glad."

THE MOUNTAIN

RIDING MYARK UP THE rocky plains was excruciating. Each time the steed's feet struck the ground, it sent shock waves of pain up Abriel's leg. He had been able to stifle his moaning, but he was in tremendous physical anguish. He hardly noticed when the terrain began pitching upward at the base of the mountain.

Thunder continued to direct the expedition through Abriel's hand. He translated Thunder's motions into instructions Myark could understand. All of this was second nature by now, but the pain had not become commonplace yet. Abriel did not regret his noble act, but he questioned whether he could endure the pain. He had the opportunity to be healed, but in an attempt to honor his visitor, he had refused. The honor was mixed with the brashness of the decision now. He hoped above all that the King was pleased with him.

Myark climbed steadily upward as the ground grew increasingly more rigid. The clop of his feet sounded and echoed around them as if there were ten more steeds in tow. All of the other animals that had been following long since had fallen behind, save a few birds that still circled high above. Estra was the only one who had been able to keep up with Myark's incredible speed.

Although Abriel consciously realized that they were climbing the mountain, he could hardly enjoy the victory. The sickening torture that his broken leg offered him made it impossible to enjoy anything. The whole thing had exhausted him so extremely that he felt as if he could fall off of Myark and wither away. His mood had grown increasingly sullen the further they rode. Abriel felt a sense of purpose go out of him as the hours passed.

Thunder nudged Abriel's hand. Abriel tugged Myark's mane. Myark corrected his course. The trip continued this way for the afternoon. With every step, he grew more discouraged. He wasn't sure what to do, but he wasn't feeling himself.

"Have we almost arrived?" Abriel said to Thunderfoot. As expected, the turtle didn't respond but simply sat still. It frustrated Abriel to be ignored. He lifted his guide up from where he had been sitting between Myark's shoulders. Holding the turtle up to his face, Abriel tried again.

This time, he mouthed the words slowly with deliberate volume.

"Are we nearly there?"

Thunder stretched out his neck as if he were going to bite the hand that held him. When he didn't, Abriel took another breath as if he were going to repeat his question. Before he could speak, Thunder dropped an unfriendly gift on Abriel's hand.

"How dare you poop on me!" Abriel groaned. He slung his hand in hopes of getting it clean.

"Stop," Abriel shouted to Myark. The steed seemed to understand much better than Thunder did. With an abrupt halt that nearly toppled Abriel over the front end of the steed, the expedition came to a standstill. Abriel huffed. He was quite put out. He was ready to get down from Myark's back but was too impatient to wait for the trompsteed to kneel. He leaned to one side in order to dismount as he had many times before.

As soon as he did, he realized his mistake. A sharp, powerful pain shot up his broken leg as he tried to right his leaning. Abriel lost his grip on Myark and tumbled to the side. The ground was hard where he hit. The fall wouldn't have hurt all that bad, but owing to his fracture, it was as close to unbearable as he could imagine.

He shouted out with a scream that made Myark jump. He and Estra both turned and stepped in close to where Abriel lay in a heap on the ground. Tears poured from his face as the uncontrollable agony grew. He gripped his leg, but it did not help. The steeds knelt down, wishing to offer aid, but there was nothing they could do. Abriel's cries carried far and wide across the hard rock surface of the mountain.

Something was wrong with his body. His heart raced too fast. His skin became clammy, and his breathing was quick and shallow. He could not catch his breath no matter how fast he gulped for air. Between the cries of pain and the short staccato breaths he noticed that something was wrong with his eyes. He blinked as he tried to understand. Around the edges of his vision black seemed to be creeping in.

So focused on the pain, he could hardly tell what was happening to him. The darkness narrowed his sight down little by little until blackness took him over. Unconsciousness covered him like a thick blanket as his natural defense against panic calmed his body with forced sleep. He passed out and lay there until dusk.

A FLOWER

THE FIRST THING ABRIEL noticed when he awoke was singing. He wondered if Myark or Estra had found a voice. His head lay on something soft which was also strange. He specifically remembered resting on the rock where he had fallen. Something was touching him. No not just touching, but petting. Something like fingers were being run through his hair as a voice hummed a little, enchanting melody.

He wondered if he could be dreaming. He ventured a peek through slit eyelids. The sky was amber and gold along the distant horizon. He looked out over the far country from where he lay on the mountain. He turned his head to take in the full view. As he did, the singing stopped. The soft something under his head shifted slightly.

Now, almost silhouetted against the evening sky, a face came into view. He said nothing but simply let his eyes trace the features. A smile stretched across the smooth skin. The eyes looked back. They were human eyes, as was the face, but it was unlike any he had ever seen. It was soft. It was kind. It was pleasing. He let himself stare for a long moment without feeling the need to arise.

"I heard you shouting, and came here to find you lying on the ground," came a musical voice. It was like the song of a bird. The voice was not so different from his own or his garden brothers, but it had a smoother quality. "I couldn't let you lie there with your head against the rocks. I was afraid you would wake with a frightful headache."

Abriel continued to smile at the face, partially wondering if he should get up. Again, he felt a hand playing with his hair. Within another second, the singing resumed. Abriel studied the features of this person. What was different? The age was similar to his, but the features seemed to imply something unknown to Abriel. *Less angular,* he thought as he tried to puzzle it together. Abriel did not sit up but spoke from where he lay in the lap of the stranger.

"What type of creature are you?" Abriel asked. He didn't know how else to form the question. It sounded strange coming from his mouth, but it was as good as he could do.

"I was wondering the same thing about you."

There was something so incredibly pleasing about the face. He reached up, almost without thinking, and touched the cheek of the stranger. He spoke absently as he felt the smooth skin there. He was having a hard time keeping his mind on the conversation.

"Teacher said that there are no other boys in Newearth."

"What is a boy?" said the melodic voice. Confusion crossed Abriel's face. This was quite unexpected.

"I am a boy, as are my brothers," Abriel said. He wondered if it was possible that this stranger was no boy at all. He could almost believe it. The features he saw did not fit into the definition he had in his mind.

"I am a girl."

It felt as if Abriel's stomach was twisting into knots with each word. He didn't know what girl meant, but he liked the sound of it. He had barely blinked since he first looked at her face and could easily continue to stare.

Placing his hands on the ground next to him, he sat up. Reluctant to look away, he glanced around. His two trompsteed friends were nearby, grazing on what little plant life grew there. He assumed Thunder was nearby as well.

He turned his attention back to the girl. Now seeing her whole form, he hardly felt like he could contain himself. His heart was trying to crawl up into his throat. His hungry eyes drank in the sight as orange shafts of dusk light streamed in from the west. He let his eyes linger first on her face, then on her body as she waited for him to respond.

"I've never seen anything like-" he started to say, but then lost his train of thought. She smiled, which nearly sent him into a coma. He didn't know what was happening, but it was absolutely intoxicating. He wondered if it would be ok to touch her more.

She had long, dark hair that fell around her shoulders and danced in the light breeze. Her skin was as smooth as the surface of a pond in the morning. Behind one ear, she had tucked a yellow flower. He stared at the flower. It stood as a reminder of his task. He briefly wondered if this girl could join him on his mission. He hoped with everything that she would come with him.

He adjusted himself thinking that he would stand up when he sensed something peculiar. He reached down to his leg as he realized that the pain there had lessened. He tapped it, and found that it was numb to the touch. He glanced back to the girl as she spoke.

"How did you numb the pain?" Abriel asked.

"I don't know about this thing you call pain. When we were in the garden," She paused to rephrase. "I mean, when we were in our garden, we used the petals of the polyfrond flower to help us sleep. I found some and gave you some while you were unconscious. Although you were asleep, you were not peaceful."

She said this all as she gestured to the flower behind her ear. He grinned and then looked back at his leg. Impossibly, his affections for the girl grew even greater. What was he going to do with these immeasurable feelings?

Trying to put his thoughts in order, he realized that he had not introduced himself, something that was rarely needed on Newearth.

"I'm Abriel."

"Abriel," she repeated as if trying it out. Abriel waited, expecting her to share her name as well. When she didn't, he spoke up again.

"What is your name?"

"I do not have one yet," the girl said. "Teacher said we would someday meet our name giver."

Abriel's eyes got wide. He leaned in, grasping something familiar in her words. His volume was too loud, but it made the girl giggle.

"You know, Teacher, Oscar?" Abriel said.

"No, my teacher's name is Saphira."

"Oh," Abriel said, a little confused. "And are there others like you?"

"Of course," she responded. "There are eleven others."

It was all so strange to find out that there was another place where twelve girls were learning from another teacher. He wished he could take the time to understand but it was beginning to get dark. He thought he should find a place for them to sleep for the night. The rocks were not very comfortable.

As he stood, he was surprised to find that he could put a little weight on his leg. It was not healed by any means, but there was at least temporary relief. He reached out his hand and offered it to the girl to help her up.

"What should I call you?" he asked. She didn't have a name, but he thought it would be strange to call her "girl." Once she was on her feet, she spoke softly.

"Teacher called us each by the name of a flower. She said we would someday get our forever names, but until then, we should be called something that will come and go as the flowers do, and as they grow, so shall I." She leaned in close as she said, "I am called Zinnia, for now."

Abriel felt as if he could melt. Her voice was like a cool running stream that watered a thirsty forest. It sent shivers up his back. He reached for her hands as he looked again at her features. He could have shouted with the extreme joy of it all.

For a long few moments, he stared into her eyes. Being with her was somehow right. There was nothing else that could possibly feel so good. Although, there was a small concern in the back of his mind. He wanted to ignore it, but he knew he could not.

He had been sent to this very mountain with a mission. He had a purpose, and he knew as silly as it seemed in light of recent developments, he had to stay focused. With tremendous determination he found the will to press on.

Holding her hand, he said, "Will you come with me?"

"Of course. Where are we going?" she asked.

"My teacher has sent me on a task, and I must complete it." Abriel said as he began to walk.

She let him direct her as they held hands. She leaned in close as they stepped over rocks and maneuvered around boulders. Myark and Estra lifted their heads to see what was happening. Zinnia questioned him idly.

"What is the task?"

"I am to find a flower on this mountain. I am to name it and help it grow," he said. As soon as she heard the words, she planted her feet. Still holding her hand, she let the slack in their arms run out. When Abriel felt her hand pull on his, he turned to see why she had stopped.

"Look around, Abriel. There is nothing that can grow among these rocks except shrubs."

"I know it seems impossible, but it is my task," Abriel said with as much strength as he had. Truthfully, he wanted to give up the search and rest there with Zinnia, but he was determined to do what he was sent to do. She tugged on his hand to pull him closer.

"Silly, I don't mean to say it's impossible. I mean to say that you are already holding the flower you came for." She let the words sink in as she watched his face. It took longer than it probably should have, but he had come a long way, and it seemed too good to be true. A smile began to break across his face.

"Do you think that's what Teacher meant?" Abriel asked. He wanted it to be true. Zinnia squeezed his hand as she responded.

"I don't know your teacher, but Sapphira, my teacher, often speaks in riddles. It seems like something a teacher might do."

Abriel thought about it for another moment as he let his eyes wander the perfect lines of her face once more. He laughed as he responded.

"Yes, Oscar is very much like that as well."

"My darling boy, I will go wherever you wish. We can search every single step of this mountain if you want. I don't mind. I can tell you, though, I've been on this mountain for a long time, and there are no flowers but me."

After a moment of contemplation his world began to make sense. The days of travel had seemed so many before the trip, but he would have done a million more if he would have known this was the flower that waited at the end of the journey. He marveled at his teacher's way of getting him here.

He let go of her hand and stepped forward. Wrapping his arms around her, he lifted her up off the ground and spun around. He thought nothing of his broken leg. He had been wanting to do it since he'd seen her. He had wondered how it would feel. It felt great. She fit him perfectly. Their complementary lines meshed together as one shape. He could not believe the beauty and magic of the encounter. As he spun her around, he whispered a prayer.

"Thank you, my King."

ARC

ABRIEL LED ZINNIA AND the various animals that followed them to a place to lie down for the night. He had picked a high cliff that looked out over a great distance. The land of the rocky valley below pressed up against the foundation of the mountain below them. At their great height, he could see the grassland beyond and even the hazy line of the forest before the horizon overtook the landscape.

The view made him feel powerful and proud of the journey he had made. He had chosen the high cliff to sleep on because the morning light would prove to be majestic. After smoothing a place for Zinnia to lie he nestled close to her through the night. The wind that gusted up from the rocky face below was frigid, but it served as a chance to hold her close. Myark, and Estra slept nearby as did Thunderfoot.

For Abriel, the world was alive with excitement and mystery. He didn't know what the King's plan for him and Zinnia was, but he knew it would be fantastic. He could hardly wait for the next morning to come so that they could begin their next adventure together. Newearth had changed for Abriel the moment he had seen her. He had dreamed of going to the Great City for so long that he could hardly remember wanting anything else. Now that his desires had changed, he didn't think of the Holy City.

He wondered if sleep would come at all. He was too excited to drift off. Instead, he thought about what he would name Zinnia. It had to be something special. It couldn't be as simple as the names he had given the beasts. He needed something delicate, but strong. He whispered possible names to himself as his flower slept in his arms. Nothing sounded right.

For no reason he could understand, he suddenly felt like he was being watched. A strange tingle began to creep up his back as the hairs stood on end. Trying not to disturb Zinnia where she slept, Abriel sat up to look around. It was dark but for the stars. Wide-eyed, he looked behind where they were lying. The trompsteeds were sleeping quietly. Thunder was hidden by the darkness, since he looked so much like a rock when he slept.

Near where Myark was sleeping, Abriel thought he saw something. He got very still and tried to look through the thick blanket of night. It was something like a disturbance in the air. A shadow was beginning to stretch out from a single point. He leaned in to get a better view. Looking toward it made his heart race. He had never seen anything like it.

As the disturbance grew, it expanded outward like a dark cloud, but as it did, it obscured what little was visible behind. The shadow swelled until it was about the size of Abriel. It was hard to get a sense of the shape since it was already so dark. It was as if whatever light should have reflected from the object was not allowed to escape.

After a moment, the dark shadow began to move. Abriel immediately shot to his feet, wondering if he would need to protect Zinnia from the dark silhouette. Some of the effects of the polyfrond flower had worn off. He felt a mild tinge of pain in his thigh. He ignored it. With its apparent movement, he could see that the shadow was roughly shaped like a man, but a man of immense size. The black-hole like figure stepped silently toward them. Abriel tensed, not knowing what he was expected to do. The dark specter was eerie. The sensation of danger was new to Abriel, but deep inside, he could feel that he needed to be on his guard. His muscles were stretched tight.

The night shadow continued forward so smoothly that it felt like each step lasted a thousand years, and only an instant at the same time. With fists clenched and legs ready to spring, Abriel whispered. He didn't want to wake Zinnia, but he also didn't want the shadow to get too close.

"What do you want?" Abriel asked in a quiet voice. The shadow stopped and stood still for a long moment before it spoke.

"There is no need to whisper. I have caused the woman to fall into a deep sleep."

Abriel looked back at Zinnia. He did not like the idea of this shadow causing anything to happen to his beloved flower. Still tense and ready Abriel spun back toward the darkness. He was startled to find that it was close enough to touch when he turned back. He let out an involuntary gasp when he realized how close the darkness was. Out of nervousness, he spoke again.

"Who are you?"

With a violent leap, the shadow lunged forward. There was no sound, but the thump of Abriel's pulsing heart. He put out his hands to stop the thrust, but it did nothing. In a fraction of a second, the cloud of darkness had surrounded him. He reached out, trying to find his way free, but it was no use. He stepped backward, but the darkness still enveloped him.

As he groped in the cloud of shadow he noticed that it was not all dark, in fact there was light that began to grow. As each moment passed the illumination grew brighter. Abriel tried to see his hand in front of his face, but the light did strange things. It didn't illuminate his skin as expected. His hand formed a dark silhouette against the growing wall of light. The voice, now powerful and immersive spoke.

"My light is for me alone. It is under my command only."

Abriel looked down at his body, and the same was true. The light that flooded all around him bent and twisted so that it didn't touch his skin. The nebulous cloud of darkness had converted to pure light, but the light was unnatural and twisted somehow. Abriel was uncomfortable with the arrangement. He turned his attention to the glowing cloud around him.

"Why have you come?" Abriel asked.

"I have come to save you."

"From what are you saving me?"

"From this beast."

Suddenly a tendril of light stretched out and encircled Zinnia where she was sleeping nearby. The light seemed to flow like a river, splashing tumultuously around the figure of the girl. Abriel felt intense emotion rise in his throat.

"That is no beast," Abriel said. He let his voice break off into a low growl. He then added, "She is under my protection."

"And you are under *my* protection, which is why I have come. I am here to save you from being undone."

The cloud of twisted light began to fade away. The light slowly solidified in front of Abriel. He was relieved that the cloud that had enveloped him shrank away. In its place the form of a person, near the size of Abriel remained. Under only the shimmer of the stars now this shadowy figure stood face to face. Abriel could feel his muscles ease and the tension melt away.

"What are you called?" Abriel said to the man in front of him.

"I have been called many things, but to you, my name is Arc." Abriel noticed that Arc's voice sounded similar to his own. He had transformed into a boy. As he looked, he realized that he was a boy close to Abriel's own age. There was something comforting about having another boy there. It reminded him of his garden brothers.

"I do not mean to disrespect you, Arc. However, I think you are confused. It is my mission to protect Zinnia, not to be protected from her."

"My friend, is it not you who are confused?" Arc reached out and placed a friendly hand on Abriel's shoulder. He turned him so that they could look at Zinnia. She still slept peacefully near the edge of the cliff. Abriel let his eyes trace her attractive lines. When he realized that he had lost himself in the vision, he looked to Arc, who was staring at him.

"Even now, you are being enchanted by her dark magic," Arc continued. "You can feel it, can't you. She is making you her servant. You are not entirely in control of yourself any longer. It has begun; she has taken your thoughts hostage."

Abriel thought about his words. It was true that he had felt different since the moment he had seen her. Certain things within his mind and body had awoken. He had been having thoughts that he had never imagined to think before. He had found himself thinking about her almost every second since he had seen her.

"I can see a kind of truth in what you say, but it is a pleasant kind of change," Abriel said.

"That is the darkness of her magic. If she had taken over your mind by force, then you would know that you were a captive. Instead, she takes over your mind and body so insidiously that you are unaware that she is doing it. You probably feel as if she is what you want, don't you?"

Abriel thought about what Arc said for a few seconds before he responded. Although he didn't want to admit it, he recognized that he could not falsify Arc's words. He could not prove that it wasn't some dark magic. He gave a little ground as he admitted Arc's words to be true with a nod.

"What am I to do about it?" Abriel asked.

"You are to make her your servant, before she makes you hers. Otherwise, you will live in a perpetual state of servitude. Every day of your life will be spent thinking about what is best for her, not yourself. A terrible prison comes with being a servant."

Abriel considered the words. He could see the truth in it, but it was like looking at the half light of the Great City through the branches of the unnamed tree. Some light was getting through, but it was not all of the light. There was a truth to the words, but it was not the whole truth.

Abriel thought back to his days in the garden with his teacher. He thought of the lessons he had learned from Oscar. One particular moment stood out to him. A moment in which Oscar taught him an important lesson. It was as if suddenly he could see the whole light, unblocked by the branches. He relayed his counterpoint victoriously.

"Teacher told me that I am in this world to serve, not to be served. If I am to be Zinnia's servant, then I accept that mission. Teacher Oscar has said it, so I trust his words,"

Abriel said. Apparently, Arc was not going to be persuaded so easily.

"As you said, she has changed you, taking from you what you have always wanted. You have desire to visit the Great City. She has forced you to change. This is a dangerous kind of magic to be sure."

It was true. For years, Abriel had wanted more than anything else to see the Great City for himself. There was nothing that had dominated his desires so much. However, from the moment he had seen Zinnia, he had not thought about it at all. It was a little disconcerting how quickly the landscape of his thoughts had changed.

"How can I continue to desire good things for myself, and desire good things for her?" Abriel asked. Arc was quick this time, jumping at the question as if he had anticipated it.

"You must leave her and go to the Great City. It is what you have wanted. You will see that once you are away from her, her magic has no power on you from a distance. You must follow your dreams. I can show you the way to the Great City."

Abriel marveled at this. How did Arc know the way? He wondered if this was his teacher's plan. His teacher had promised him a visit to the Great City if he accepted the mission to the mountain. He imagined leaving Zinnia where she was sleeping and making his way to the Great City with Arc. He knew it would be a marvelous trek. He knew that the Great City would not disappoint.

He thought about his own trip. For most of the journey, he had wanted nothing more than for it to be over. He had only wanted to go to the Great City, but because of Thunderfoot's persistent stubbornness, Abriel had learned an incredibly valuable lesson. Again with victory in his voice, Abriel announced his conclusion.

"My guide taught me that what I want is not always what I need. I wanted one thing, but at the end of the journey, I realized that what I needed was something different. Once my journey was complete, I came to understand that what I received for the journey was greater by far than what I thought I wanted in the first place. So if she changes what I thought I wanted, I accept that."

This time, Abriel was quite proud of his defense. However, he was beginning to see that this exchange was not going to be won easily. Arc came back with words more emphatic than any he had used so far. His voice was stronger and more urgent than before. This time, Arc pointed to Abriel's leg as he spoke.

"Do you remember the pain of your broken leg?"

"Of course, how could I forget?"

"This is what waits for you if you stay with this beastly woman. I have seen it before in the previous Earth. It was the first mother who bent that world until it was a place of pain and suffering. For generations, her descendants lived in utter torment because of that woman's selfish act. You can not take such a risk here. By allowing her to live, you are dooming this world to an endless cycle of pain. After all, was it not in coming to her that you experienced this great pain in your leg? This is only the beginning."

Arc's words hit him like a fall from a tall tree. He felt as if his breath had been sucked from his body. Although he tried, he could not find a crack in the logic. He had heard stories of the previous world from his teacher. It was clear that Arc was right, but Abriel fought the notion with all of his mental strength. He looked for an angle that he could use to defend his position, but he found himself becoming convinced.

Teacher had taught him and his garden brothers that the worst thing that could happen is for Newearth to become bent. Above all, he had to avoid that. Beyond that, it scared him greatly to imagine having to endure the pain. He thought of the moments after he had fallen and broken his leg. The agony was so impossibly horrid that he could not allow that to happen to others. Not only for himself but for the others who would inhabit Newearth, he realized that he had to do something to stop this risk.

"What must I do?" Abriel asked.

"See where she lies there?" Arc pointed to where she was sleeping. Abriel nodded. "Simply push her body off of the ledge and this nightmare will be avoided."

"You want me to push her off the cliff, will she not feel great pain as I did?" Abriel asked. He did not want to hurt her.

"No," Arc said confidently. "This cliff is much higher than the one you fell from. She will not feel pain. This cliff is high enough to kill her."

"Kill her? What is kill?" Abriel asked. He had never heard the word. It had a kind of odd taste in his mouth as he said it.

"Kill is to end. It will end the risk for this world. You will be doing the world a great favor by doing this service."

Abriel walked to her slowly, feeling a strange kind of daze. It felt somewhat like a dream. His body was moving, but he wasn't entirely sure that he had full control. He stared down at her as she slept. He could not allow the world to be plunged into such pain and suffering as the previous world had been. He knelt down and kissed her on the forehead. Still, she slept. He placed his hands on her, readying himself. He held his breath and tensed his muscles. He began to push but then paused.

"I should ask the King," Abriel said. With speed like lightning, Arc was next to him. Arc put his hands on Abriel's and applied pressure.

"The King is busy. He has many things he must do. Do not bother him with this simple task. One shove and it will be done."

Abriel felt embarrassed. How could he have thought it would be OK to bother the King with this? Arc was right, the King was impossibly high and mighty. Why should he waste the King's time? Although it still seemed strange. Abriel tried to remember if Oscar or the King had said anything about killing.

Abriel could not remember anything that Oscar had said on the subject. His mind felt sluggish as if he were trudging through waist deep mud. With a great deal of effort he turned his mind toward the King trying to remember anything he had said about killing.

He could feel Arc pushing his hands toward the edge of the cliff. Zinnia's limp body rolled over toward the ledge. Abriel recounted his meeting with the King. He thought about what he was told. He was now certain that there was no mention of killing, but one phrase from the King did stand out. Abriel stepped back from Zinnia and shoved Arc as well.

"The King told me, receiving something of great value is worth enduring great pain," Abriel said.

He glanced at Arc. Something like fog cleared from around him. His mind flexed and pushed back the shadowy influence. The daze of darkness that had clouded his mind disappeared, and Abriel could see with deep clarity. *How could I have listened to his twisted words*, he wondered.

He felt a knot in his stomach as he looked at the dark visitor. He had almost been convinced that this stranger had his interest in mind. Abriel tightened as it occurred to him that Arc was capable of speaking untruth. Like a blast of light to Abriel's mind, he felt something powerful flow into his body.

Arc had been enchanting him somehow. Abriel steeled himself as if readying for a fight. He determined that he would not listen to anything else Arc had to say. It was Arc, not Zinnia, who was the twister of truth. Abriel clenched his jaw, ready.

"You have misunderstood," Arc began. This time, it was Abriel who took control. He thought back to the many times that Thunderfoot had shown his stubbornness. Abriel looked down at his hand, where his turtle guide had bitten him over and over. This stubborn act of defiance gave Abriel an idea.

As Arc tried to continue, Abriel leaned in and bit him. Arc stopped what he was saying for a brief moment as Abriel sank his teeth into the skin of his arm. He released him almost as quickly. Arc acted as if he did not notice. He started again.

"Abriel, listen to me. I'm here to protect-"

Abriel cut him off by biting him again. This time, he sank his teeth into Arc's arm. He began to see why Thunderfoot used this tactic. It was strongly satisfying. He released his clenched jaw and stepped back.

"You won't get another chance like this, I promise-"

Once more, Abriel used his teeth to demonstrate his defiance. This time, he bit down hard, trying to communicate his message more clearly. He forced his teeth into the skin. Although Abriel assumed that the body before him was only an illusion, he let his bite go and leaned back.

To his surprise. Arc was gone. Abriel was proud of his victory. He looked around him. The trompsteeds were still sleeping. Thunderfoot was still hidden away somewhere. He took a deep breath and said, "Thank you for the strength to overcome."

After whispering his prayer, he sat up for a while thinking about what had just happened. He then lay down next to Zinnia and nestled in close. He was so happy to have vanquished Arc that he could have shouted for joy, but he didn't want to wake Zinnia.

She sighed a little as he wrapped his arms around her sleeping body. It felt like home.

ONCE AGAIN

ABRIEL AWOKE TO THE sound of talking. It was Zinnia's voice he heard first. When he came to, he realized that she was no longer in his arms. He sat up and glanced around. Zinnia was sitting nearby, talking to Arc. She was deeply engaged in the conversation. Abriel rose and rushed over to her.

"Zinnia, don't listen to him, he doesn't speak the truth," Abriel said. Zinnia glanced at him, but it was clear that she was torn. She had been listening to him for some time, apparently, because the look on her face was one of confusion. Arc cut in.

"Ahh, the slothful man awakes," Arc said. His voice was raw and accusatory. Abriel looked to Arc but determined that he would ignore him. Arc directed his next comment at Zinnia. "As I was saying, I tried to talk to Abriel, but he bit me mercilessly. Not just once but three times. I thought that I should warn you about him."

Arc leaned in close from where he was sitting to show Zinnia the teeth marks on his arm. Zinnia touched them and looked up to Abriel as if to ask if it was true. There was hurt in her eyes. She could not believe that Abriel would be so violent. Abriel tried to defend himself.

"It's not like that, he was not speaking the truth. I was just doing what Thunderfoot taught me-" Arc cut Abriel off as he spoke to Zinnia.

"That is my point exactly. It is dangerous for you to be near this beastly man. If he is willing to act like a beast, how do you know he will not try to bite you as well?" Arc was saying when Abriel tried to cut in.

"Now wait a minute, stop this. You are not telling the full truth," Abriel said, trying to explain. Zinnia reached up to touch Abriel on the arm as she spoke.

"Is it true that you bit him?"

"Well, that part is true, but he was-"

"So you see," Arc cut in. "Is it possible that he is more beast than he is man?"

Abriel knelt down and took Zinnia's hands. He looked her in the eyes as he spoke with as much confidence as he had. He said, "I promise I won't treat you that way. I was trying to protect you. Maybe I was wrong to bite him, I don't know. I feel very confused. I won't bite you."

As soon as Abriel finished, Arc took back Zinnia's attention. He said, "Let me ask you a question, young lady. What do you want from this man?"

Zinnia thought about it for a long moment. Abriel was clearly interested in the answer to that question as well, so he waited. Zinnia came up with an answer and spoke it to them both.

"Companionship."

"Not a servant?" Arc asked. She shook her head to indicate that that was not what she wanted from the relationship.

"Ahh, I see," Arc said, but then added, "That really is too bad."

"What is too bad?" Zinnia asked. Abriel did not see where Arc was going with this line of reasoning, so he waited to hear Arc's answer.

"Abriel's mission in life is to be a servant. He told me so himself. I'm sorry. From his own mouth, he admits he can not be what you want," Arc said as he leaned back against a rock to let the statement sink in. Clearly, Zinnia was confused. Abriel chimed in once more.

"Now hold on-" he began to say, but Arc cut him off using his own words against him. He pitched and imitated Abriel's voice so perfectly that it was uncanny.

"I am in this world to serve, not to be served," he said. He then gave commentary on Abriel's words. "So you see, he does not desire to be your equal, which is required of a companion. Instead, he would place himself below you and be your servant. He aims to be something other than what you want."

Abriel tried to cut in, but Arc was too quick. He turned it back on Abriel and asked, "Aren't those the words you used?" He was reluctant to answer this time. He wished it could all slow down so he could think. Arc was too quick to argue with.

"Well, yes, that is the words I used, but-" he was saying, but Arc cut in again.

"So you see, Zinnia, his chosen role is not what you want."

He stopped to allow Zinnia to respond, but Abriel seized the opportunity to defend himself. He interrupted what Zinnia was about to say. "That is not what I meant!" Arc barked loudly at him for interrupting.

"Now he won't let the lady speak," Arc said. This quieted Abriel. Although he wanted to defend himself, he did not want to talk over Zinnia. He waited for her to respond.

"I can see that he has said these things, but that he meant a different thing by saying them than what you say they mean," she said. Abriel celebrated inwardly. She was stronger than he had thought. She had not fallen for Arc's trick. Abriel began to speak up now.

"Arc, it is time for you to leave," Abriel said.

"I will leave if the lady bids me go, but I don't think she would want me to leave before I have told her all that you have said," Arc said and then waited for a response. Again, not wanting to interrupt Zinnia, Abriel waited for her to respond. He held his breath in hopes that she would send Arc away.

"I will hear what you have to say," she said. Abriel felt completely powerless. He felt like it would be wrong to demand of her that she send him away, but he felt like it would be wrong to do nothing. All he could do was prepare to protect her from Arc's lies.

"He told me that he does not want or need you," Arc said to Zinnia. Abriel could not control himself. He shouted out.

"I did not say that."

"Again, the man tries to stop me from speaking. Does he have something to hide?" Arc asked.

"I don't have anything to hide."

"He told me that what he wants is not what he needs. He said that he wanted one thing for a very long time, but learned that it was not what he needed. So, my dear lady, if he says that he wants you, that must mean he doesn't need you. If he says he needs you, it means that he doesn't want you. So by his own words, he neither wants you nor needs you."

"That is not true," Abriel shouted. Arc was quick to respond.

"You know that you said these words, and you can not truthfully deny them. If you say you didn't say them, you prove yourself to be a liar. If you say that you want and need Zinnia, then you make yourself a liar. If you did say them, then prove the logic false," Arc said.

Abriel tried to go back in his mind to what Arc had said. He wanted to defend himself, but he was finding it almost impossible to keep up with the stream of logic. He was beginning to understand that there was more at stake here. He could feel that Arc saw fit to tear Zinnia from him. He could not let it happen, but he didn't know how to defend the logic.

Without giving him a chance to defend himself, Arc continued. Abriel turned to Zinna and spoke to her directly.

"Please, don't listen to him. He is twisting my words," Abriel pleaded. It was no use. Arc was obviously winning, and he could do nothing to stop the onslaught. Abriel tried to convince as he said, "Zinnia, I value you above everything else. Please-" Arc cut him off again.

"Ahh, value. He told me that things of great value are worth great pain. My dear, you value Abriel greatly, don't you?" Arc asked. She nodded.

"Stop!" Abriel shouted. Both Arc and Zinnia ignored him. He could feel her slipping away.

"He told me that for things of great value, one must suffer great pain."

"What is pain?" Zinnia asked.

"Here I will show you," Arc said.

"No, don't!" Abriel shouted again. This time, Zinnia jumped. Arc seized the opportunity.

"Oh, now the man wishes to keep you ignorant," Arc said.

"No, I just-"

"What are you going to do, bite me?" Arc said.

With that Abriel turned all of his attention to Zinnia. He began pleading her with tears in his eyes, "Send him away. He is bent. He will leave us twisted. He will leave our world broken. Send him away, please."

Zinnia looked to Abriel and then to Arc. Slowly and cautiously, she reached out for Arc as he reached for her.

"Show me what pain is," she said.

Arc complied. He grabbed her hand. As soon as he did, Zinnia began to scream. She fell to the ground, but Arc did not let go. Like the wild beast that he had been accused of being, Abriel leaped for Arc. He would tear him to pieces. He would destroy him.

Abriel lunged and wrapped his arms around Arc. He swung, bit, and scratched. He punched and kicked. No matter what, he couldn't do any damage to Arc. Abriel could not understand. Zinnia writhed on the ground in pain. Her hand was still in Arc's.

Abriel set about trying to pull her hand from his. He tugged with all of his strength, trying to wrestle her arm from his grip. His strength was puny compared to Arc's. Abriel continued to fight. By now, Myark and Estra were awake and making a fury of noise. Abriel grabbed a heavy rock and smashed it over the back of Arc's head. Still, he did not budge.

After a long few minutes of fighting, Arc let go of Zinnia's hand. She continued to scream for a moment. Abriel rushed to her and wrapped his arms around her, trying to comfort her. He rocked her lightly as her screams withered to moans. After a long while, she was quiet, but still she breathed heavily. Arc stood over them like a victorious warrior. Abriel whispered to Zinnia.

"Please, Zinnia, send him away. I can't do it, you have to." After a long silence, Zinnia responded.

"Get-away-from-me" Zinnia said in a weak voice. Abriel looked up to Arc.

"You heard her, Arc, she sends you away," Abriel said.

"You're mistaken, Abriel Man, she sends you away," Arc corrected. Abriel's stomach dropped. He looked back at Zinnia, who was still in his arms. Her eyes were like fire. Again, she spoke with a weak tone.

"Get away from me, Abriel. How could you love me if you plan to cause me such pain?" she asked.

Abriel let go of her and stood. He was so furious he could not even respond. He knew he was beaten. He understood that he was no match for Arc's ability to twist. He had lost. He had lost Zinnia. It felt like he had lost everything. Still, Arc was not done.

"My lady," Arc said as he helped Zinnia up. "We can not simply let Abriel get away. Think of your sisters. Even if you send him away, what would happen if he finds your garden sisters? Think of the damage he will do to them."

Abriel could not believe what he was hearing. He tried to speak but could only get a few words out. "I wouldn't hurt-" This time, it was Zinnia who interrupted him.

"What must we do?" she said.

"We must kill him. Remember, he doesn't want or need you. All he will do is bring you pain. Simply say the word, and I will kill him for you," Arc said.

Zinnia thought about his words. Abriel was so confused his head was spinning. It was like trying to untangle the vines, but the vines were lies. He couldn't see the way out. He watched Zinnia's face. He knew what would happen if she called for his death. She would become bent. She would become twisted. Abriel could not let that happen. He made his final stand.

"I am certain that we have been fooled here. I can't say why, and I can't say how, but I know that the things Arc says are not the full truth. Maybe, after all, he is right that I must die. Maybe he is right that I will bring pain. However, my sweet Zinnia, I can't allow you to make the decision. You would be bent, as the inhabitants of the former world were. It is I who must make the decision for you. You won't send him away. He will continue to try to convince you to kill me, so I will take away the option."

Abriel knelt down and kissed her on the head as he whispered to her, "I love you my flower. Believe in the King, he is the giver of life forever."

After those words, he stepped to the edge of the cliff. He spoke to Zinnia one last time. "I believe in the King. He has given me life." With that, he turned and threw himself off the cliff. He did not scream as he fell to his death. He plummeted to the rocky ground below, knowing that he had fought his hardest. He died knowing that he had done his best. He wasn't sure if he had defeated Arc, but he was

confident that he had given Zinnia everything she needed
to do so.

LEAVE

ABRIEL'S DARING ACT PULLED Zinnia out of the haze that Arc had put her under. The arguments melted away. The logic didn't matter. As she watched Abriel throw himself from the cliff, all she cared about was him. She stood and screamed as she ran to the ledge to look over.

"Abriel. No!" she shouted over and over. Her stomach twisted into a knot. She found his broken body with her eyes, far below. Something instinctual, something primal came over her. She let out another scream, but he didn't move. With a burning righteous rage, she turned on Arc.

"You beast! Leave me alone. I want nothing to do with you."

She turned her back on him and began to look for a way to climb down from the ledge. She had to get to Abriel's body.

AWAKE

ABRIEL'S EYES SHOT OPEN. He filled his lungs with a mighty heave. The air was sweet. He looked around, trying to understand where he was. His memories came back with a quick flow of consciousness. He recounted the last image he had seen.

He realized that his body was tingling. It was beyond pleasant. He closed his eyes again as the sensation of warmth soaked through to his bones. He felt amazing. He felt fresh. He felt new. He had just been reborn.

Opening his eyes again, he took in more of his location. He was in an enclosed space, although it was large. He let his eyes work their way down from the high vaulted ceiling. Gracefully arranged vines weaved along the architecture. Abriel had never been indoors, nor had he ever even conceived of such an idea.

All of the interior of the room was lined with an array of wonderfully decorated patterns. Gold and Ivory mingled together with the green plant life. The interior garden, however, was more than only plants. He would have continued to admire the architecture but something caught his eye.

Next to where he lay, which he could now see was a raised surface, stood Zinnia. Her eyes were as wide as the world. She remained quiet, but across her face grew an almost impossible expression. He felt like he would melt in the incredible warmth of her smile. Her longing gaze was as much as Abriel could have asked for. He was about to reach for Zinnia when a voice pulled him from his stare.

"He's awake," Oscar said.

Abriel turned his head the other way and saw his teacher and friend, Oscar. Abriel had missed him tremendously. He sat up straight away.

"Teacher!" Abriel said. It was almost too extraordinary to take in. He reached his hand out for Oscar from where he lay on the table. His teacher took it warmly. Abriel felt so deeply satisfied in that moment that he could have lived in it for years. When Oscar released his hand, Abriel turned his attention and reached for Zinnia. She, too, held his hand. He wanted to hold on to her forever, but there were too many questions. Before he could ask, Zinnia gestured to a woman who was standing in the room with them.

"This is my teacher, Sapphira," Zinnia said. Abriel smiled at her. She was a stately looking Elvangaleen. He turned back to Oscar.

"Where are we?" Rather than answering directly, Oscar smiled.

"I told you I would bring you here," Oscar let the words sink in as he waited for him to understand. A huge grin stretched across Abriel's face as it became clear.

"The Holy City?"

Oscar nodded. Abriel tried to sit up from the table but found himself wrapped in something. Only his arms were free from the compress. His body was still tingling, which he thought might have something to do with the material that was wrapped around him.

He reached for the wrap that his body was swaddled in and ran his fingers along its fuzzy surface. He discovered that it was not material at all, but instead a leaf so large it covered him entirely. He had never seen a leaf so enormous. It had a reddish-green tint and a supple leathery feel.

"What kind of tree-" Abriel began to say. The pattern on the leaf was incredibly delicate. He traced its lines with his fingers. He tried to imagine the plant that could have produced such a leaf. It had to be the size of a mountain.

"Come, we must be on our way. We have to get to the coronation," Oscar said. Abriel had never heard the word before, but it had a certain kind of pomp to it. He slid the leaf back as he spun to put his feet on the floor. He reached for his leg, expecting pain to explode from the break. Once he pulled back the leaf, he realized that his leg was fine. No, it was better than fine. It was completely whole. Abriel looked at Oscar, trying to understand.

"The King has given the leaves of the tree of life some incredible properties. They are for the healing of the nations," Oscar said as he patted Abriel on the back. Abriel could have asked a thousand questions for every statement that Oscar made, but there was apparently no time.

Abriel grabbed Zinnia's hand as Oscar and Saphira ushered them toward an opening in the room. Abriel looked around quickly as they walked. He didn't want to miss any of the sights and sounds that the Holy City had to offer.

Once they were through the doorway, another great hall of enormous size met his eyes. This one was twice as stunning. Its walls stretched up into the sky itself. Shafts of golden light poured down from somewhere high up. He could have stood and admired its beauty for days.

In this room, Oscar was met by a number of other people. Their glow let Abriel know that they were also Elvangaleen. Oscar spoke to them each quickly. There was an urgency and importance to his instructions, although Abriel did not understand them.

"Prepare the steeds for the Prince and Princess," Oscar instructed.

One of those that followed along as they walked peeled off, presumably to do as he was instructed. They continued their forward motion through the giant hall. Abriel was feeling overwhelmed with the high speed action that was taking place around them. Oscar turned to another as they continued to walk quickly.

"Send word that the Prince and Princess are beginning the coronation processional."

Another of the Elvangaleen split off from the small crowd and took another direction. Abriel couldn't understand what was going on, but it was fantastically exciting.

They passed through a number of other rooms, halls, and passageways. Each seemed greater and more enormous than the last. Abriel's eyes were not trained for architecture, but he enjoyed it just the same. Many times, he looked at Zinnia, who still held his hand. They would coo and make sounds of awe at the incredible sights. After Oscar had given out instructions to most of the crowd that attended him, Abriel turned toward his teacher.

"I did not imagine that the Great City would be this beautiful," Abriel said. His teacher laughed and patted his shoulder.

"My dear Abriel, you have not seen the Great City yet; this is only my house."

"House?" Abriel asked after glancing at Zinnia to see if she understood. Clearly, neither of them did.

"Oh yes, right. I mean to say this is my personal garden that the King has given me."

Abriel could hardly continue walking and take in the idea at the same time. *How could that be,* he thought. He had many more questions, but he didn't speak for the next few minutes as they continued to walk. He wondered at the size and grandeur of Oscar's mansion.

"Are all houses like this?" Zinnia asked.

"No, some are much smaller. Some are much larger." After walking through another two rooms, Oscar stopped them both and spoke quickly. "So, this will probably be pretty exciting. There are many who have come to see the coronation. I will be with you the whole way."

With that, Oscar turned toward the wall that stood in front of them. To his surprise, the wall began to move. It split down the middle and slid out of the way. Abriel had never seen a door before, but he quickly understood its purpose. Still holding hands, Abriel and Zinnia stepped into the blast of light that poured down from outside.

PARADE

THE SOUND THAT MET their ears made them both jump. The volume of a million voices filled the open air. They looked out over a sea of faces, hardly able to take in the scene. The massive crowd cheered with a fervor that Abriel could not understand. He scanned the crowd from the front steps of Oscar's palace. Strangely, the crowd was not all on ground level. Hundreds floated in the air above where they stood. They both looked back at Oscar and Sapphira, trying to understand.

"What's going on?" Abriel asked Oscar, having to shout over the noise of the cheering audience.

"They have come to celebrate your coronation."

Abriel wanted to ask more questions, but he was caught up in the moment. He looked out at the throng of Elvangaleen. Some waved flags and banners, others shouted and clapped. Abriel looked to one waving a flag. On it was the image of a crest made up of a turtle and a horse. It reminded him of Thunderfoot and his trompsteed friends. He wondered briefly what had happened to them.

He didn't know what he was supposed to do next. After a moment, he realized that the crowd was beginning to split. Coming from somewhere to the right, a path was being made. "Make way," some shouted. The cry echoed as others repeated it. As the pathway sprang from the sea of faces, he caught sight of something that gave him yet another jolt of incredible joy.

The crowd was parting for his friends, Myark and Estra, the trompsteeds. Now he cheered himself. He could have cried at the sight of them. He looked at Zinnia, who also cheered with him. They approached slowly with a deliberate cadence to their step. They looked different than they had the last time he saw them. There was a green sash that was tied around each of their necks. Their mane had been braided down their length. There was an Emerald green material that was draped over both of their backs. On it was the crest he had seen before.

The path through the crowd continued until Myark and Estra stood at the base of the steps. Now with them standing so close he saw that Thunderfoot was riding on Myark's back, near his shoulder blades. Abriel looked back to Oscar not sure what to do.

Oscar simply gestured toward the steeds. Abriel understood. He and Zinnia began to descend the stairs before them. As soon as they did, the crowd grew quiet. Before they reached the base of the stairs, it was silent. There was the vivid crackle of anticipation in the air as Abriel and Zinnia approached their friends.

Abriel was thrilled to be reunited with the trompsteeds. He wrapped his arms around Myark, and then Estra. He picked up Thunder from Myark's back and kissed him on the shell. After dispensing his affection, he helped Zinnia to climb onto Estra's back. He then leaped with agile grace to mount Myark.

On Myark's back, Abriel and Zinnia could see over the heads of the tremendous crowd that stood on ground level. With them on their steeds, the crowd erupted with applause once more. Abriel looked toward Oscar, who had also come down the steps of his home, followed by Sapphira.

Their teachers took up a leading position in front of Myark and Estra. With a slow gait, they began to walk. The trompsteeds followed close behind. Again, the crowd of onlookers parted as they began to make their way. The steeds trotted along with their heads held high. The millions of faces that watched them fanned out so far that Abriel could not see the end of the crowd.

Now that they were on the move, Abriel and Zinnia began to take in the cityscape. His teacher had called it a city, but it was so immeasurably huge that Abriel thought it to be a world unto itself. Stretching out in every direction were exquisitely gardened estates of stupendous grandeur. Rising into the sky were shining spires of enormous beauty.

Abriel looked up into the air where many Elvangaleen were floating overhead. He let his eyes roam out past them into the open sky beyond. He had seen stars from Newearth, but never anything like the view that met his eyes here. The sky was blue and bright, but even with the brilliant daylight, an array of stars and colorful worlds shone through the illuminated atmosphere. It gave him butterflies to look at the majestic view. He wondered if he would ever be able to explore those distant depths. The sound of the crowd pulled him back to the moment.

The street that the steeds trotted along were reflective. Abriel could see their image below in the polished surface. The shining gold of the street gave everyone who stood near a magical glow as light bounced from every smooth surface.

Great trees and gardens grew at every turn. The most magnificent fruit hung on every plant that they passed. The buildings were interwoven seamlessly with the plant life. It was impossible in most cases to tell where the plants ended and the buildings began. Magnificent structures rose and wove themselves into the sky around them. They could not imagine a more beautiful place.

Abriel looked behind them and found that as they passed, the crowd would close in behind them and follow. The tremendous parade of Elvangaleen stretched out of sight. He turned back around to see that they had come to the end of the street they were on, and were now turning onto another. There waited even more people. The street was so wide that a hundred people could stand shoulder to shoulder and still not span its width. Lining each side of the great thoroughfare were so many people that it made Abriel's head spin. They, too, cheered.

Now that they were on this great street, Abriel could see that the terrain rose gradually upward. In the distance he could see that the street led toward a great mountain in the distance. On the peek of the mountain, there was an enormous shining beacon of light. He had to squint his eyes to see. There was so much light pouring out from the top of the mountain, that it seemed that the entire Holy City was illuminated from the light that came from it.

The next thing that he noticed was the splash of water. He looked down to find that the steeds were ankle deep in a crystal clear flow. As they continued forward, he could see that at the center of the massive road there was water that flowed deep and clear. Abriel wondered at this as he pointed it out to Zinnia.

They continued their approach toward the mountain, as the sound of a powerful rushing water was mingling with the noise of the cheering crowd. Abriel put his hand to his forehead to shield his eyes from the light coming off of the peak. He saw a massive river flowing done the mountain. Near the top of the mountain was a huge waterfall that spilled out onto the golden shining road.

"Where is the water coming from?" Abriel asked. He was surprised that Oscar could hear him over the noise of the crowd.

"This is the river of the water of life. It flows from the throne of the King," Oscar said.

Abriel could not quite envision how that could be, but something else had caught his attention. He thought at first that they were going into a forest that lined the river and the great street. It looked as if the forest surrounded the flowing water at the base of the mountain. As they entered underneath an enormous, lush canopy of tree tops, he realized that his impression had been wrong.

To his surprise, it was not a forest, but one single tree that grew on either side of the river. It stretched on for a great distance. He marveled at the size of the leaves from the tree. The leaf that he had been wrapped in must have come from this fantastic growth. The leaves were of all sizes, shapes, and colors. This must have been the father of all trees. It had every kind of leaf Abriel had ever seen growing there, and many that he had not.

Even more incredible than the leaves themselves was the fruit. In places, it hung low enough to reach. It had fruits of so many different colors and sizes. At different heights, different colors of fruit grew. There was fruit as big as a man in places. Abriel wanted to taste every fruit he saw, but he knew it wasn't the time.

The tree stretched up so high it seemed like it could as easily be growing down out of the sky as up from the ground. It was so big that it enveloped the entire river and the great street. The river flowed through the middle of the tree. It was parted down the center like a tunnel. It was a magical experience as their procession paraded through the middle. Being inside the tree was a world of its own. It was an entire forest's worth of branches. Some were as thick as the street itself. Abriel longed to go climbing in its massive network of limbs.

"Is this where the healing leaf came from?" Zinnia asked. Oscar made a wide gesture to the tree that now surrounded them.

"Yes, this is the Tree of Life. It bears twelve crops of fruit every month, all year long. It's beautiful, isn't it?"

They both nodded as they admired the giant Tree of Life. Abriel imagined the team of workers it would take to climb among the branches to harvest the fruit. Most of the branches were so wide that they would act as roads. As he looked closer, he realized that nestled among the tree branches and passageways were thousands more faces cheering them on as they progressed toward the mountain.

After a long walk through the center of the Tree of Life, they came out on the other side. With each step, the noise of the crowd grew louder and louder. Abriel didn't know what would wait at the end of the procession, but he could hardly stand the suspense.

On the other side of the Tree of Life they were in full view of the mountain of light. They slowed. The crowd that was gathered were all behind them now. Oscar stopped and turned to Abriel and Zinnia.

"You must go from here on foot. The mountain is the most holy place."

"Are you not coming?" Zinnia asked.

"We will watch the coronation from here," Oscar explained. After Abriel and Zinnia had climbed down from Myark and Estra, they both hugged Oscar and Sapphira.

Abriel and Zinnia turned and continued their walk up the shining street toward the mountain peak.

They walked hand in hand. They looked back a number of times as their view grew higher and higher. They could see the Holy City stretching out for as far as was possible to see. It was the most dazzling thing Abriel had ever seen. The millions of Elvangaleen that had gathered to watch had begun to grow quiet. There was an electric excitement in the air.

A GREATER MOUNTAIN

THEY TURNED AND PREPARED to take the last few steps up the mountain. It was incredibly bright. The light that poured out of the mountain top was not as ambient here. They could see that it was coming from a single point. As they drew close, they squinted trying to see the vision more clearly.

They stopped when they realized they had come to the end of the road. The mountain plateaued into a scene that was almost too much to take in. At the center of the mountain top plateau was a single point of brilliance. Radiant light poured forth from a great and mighty throne. A glowing figure sat on the throne.

Every few seconds, a bright flash of lightning would strike out from the throne, and a powerful rumble of thunder would follow. It shook the ground that they stood on. The sight filled Abriel with tremendous fear. He felt Zinnia's hand tighten around his.

Surrounding the throne was a huge crystal lake that was as smooth as glass. Abriel could now see that the throne was like an island that rose up out of the water. The water that made up the River of Life was coming from the throne. The crystal sea spread out over the whole mountain top before it flowed over the edge in a remarkable waterfall. Abriel could see that the water that came from the throne both filled this crystal sea and made up the water of the River of Life. The surface of the lake reflected the glory of the throne and the figure who sat on it.

Abriel felt like he would melt in the impossible light. He let his eyes move from the throne and saw that circling around the throne was something like an enormous rainbow of emerald light. At the edge of the crystal sea were twenty-four smaller thrones. Each of these thrones faced the main throne. On each of these sat other figures of lesser glory. They were dressed in glowing white and wore crowns of gold. Abriel marveled at the scene.

Suddenly, something else caught his attention. Near the central throne were four powerful-looking creatures floating over the water. Each somewhat resembled creatures that Abriel had seen on Newearth, but they were more fierce and terrifying than anything he'd seen. They each had six wings that flapped mightily. Somehow, the flapping of their wings did not disturb the water of the crystal sea. Stranger still, their entire bodies were covered in eyes, even under their wings. They were chanting something over and over. Each faced inward toward the main throne.

Abriel listened to the echoing voices of the four flying creatures as they chanted.

"Holy, Holy, Holy, is the Lord God Almighty, who was and is and is to come."

When the words were finished, all of the elders in the circle of thrones took their crowns off and knelt down facing the central throne. They laid their golden crowns down in honor. As if he had been in a daze, Abriel suddenly came awake. He blurted out with understanding.

"It's the King!" he said to Zinnia.

Without completely understanding, they dropped to their knees and then fell to their faces. They worshipped the King in his radiant glory for a long period of time. Many of the things that came from their mouths, they weren't even able to understand. It was impossible to tell how long they had been there, worshipping the King. It could have been minutes, it could have been centuries.

They would have been content to stay there, but at some point, the light that surrounded them changed.

"Rise," came a voice.

Abriel realized he was on his feet. He was facing the King who sat on his brilliant glowing throne. This meeting was so different than the last time he saw the King, he couldn't hardly believe it was the same King. It felt like time was stacking up on itself as the King spoke.

"Welcome to the Coronation of the Prince of Newearth!" The King said with a joyful voice. He had not shouted, but it was clear that all of the gathered throng heard his voice. The cheers from the millions who were in attendance rang out like a mighty roaring storm. Again, the King spoke. This time, Abriel knew that the King was speaking to him.

"You are the firstborn son of the chief of the twenty-four Elders. You have proven your loyalty and faithfulness to me, as your father Peter also did."

Abriel was breathing heavily. His heart felt like it would pound through his rib cage. He didn't care, nor did he notice what his body was doing. To be in the presence of the King was absolutely intoxicating.

"It is for this reason that I give you this crown."

Out of nowhere, a crown made of gold appeared on Abriel's head. It was studded with massive jewels the likes of which Abriel had never seen. He could not take his eyes off the King. Now turning to Zinnia, the King spoke.

"You are the daughter of one of the 24 elders. You have proven your loyalty and faithfulness to me, as your father Judah also did. It is for this reason that I give you this crown."

Finally, Abriel was able to look at Zinnia as a crown appeared on her head. He noted her tremendous beauty as she reflected the glory of the King, but he could not stand for his eyes to be anywhere but the High King for more than a second. Now in a louder, more powerful voice than Abriel had ever heard, the King announced, "You are to be fruitful and multiply throughout Newearth. You will show the nations how to walk by this marvelous light. The gates of this city will never be closed to you or any other who walks by this light. You, along with the other princes and princesses of Newearth, will bring your glory and honor in."

Abriel and Zinnia found themselves face down on the ground again. They worshipped the King for his generosity and miraculous mercy. Again, they were not sure how long they stayed that way. They would have been content to stay there forever, but once more the voice said, "Rise."

"Dear Prince Abriel, your flower does not have a name. It is time," the King said.

Abriel turned toward his beautiful companion. He let his eyes drink in her lovely face. It was as if he were riding on a wave. He was aware of what was happening, but it almost felt as if it was too impossible, too incredible, too extraordinary. He saw in her eyes that she felt the same. Abriel sensed that it was his time to speak.

"My lovely flower," he said as he took her hands. He didn't know how, but he could hear his voice amplified and echoing throughout the Holy City. "You are among the greatest creations of the glorious King. I will be with you as long as the King allows me to live. May we always give honor and glory to Him who is seated on the throne. Because for me, you are the beginning of a new and holy adventure, your name will be..." He paused and leaned in close as he whispered her name.

"Dawn." She smiled. Again, they were swept up by the King's radiance.

Without realizing it, they were on their faces worshiping him once more. They shouted and sang of the King's great glory and grace. Pure pleasure washed over them. They laid their crowns at his feet. They pledged themselves to the service of the King forever. Once more, his voice filled their ears.

WATCHING

OSCAR AND A HOST of powerful Elvangaleen stood at the ready. The High King had not told them what to expect but only that the time had come. Oscar had watched Abriel's procession in the shining city, but was quickly called away to prepare Newearth for its Prince and Princess. He kept his composure, but he was immeasurably proud of his student. Given an impossible situation, Abriel had done the impossible.

Oscar waited for the host to descend, knowing it would happen any moment. The sky split open and poured out celestial warriors. They had to capture Archetype of Evil; It was a direct command from the King. He would not go willingly, nor easily. Oscar's excitement bordered on fear as he anticipated the battle that would follow.

General Zath and his mighty warriors led the charge. However, this time, there were thousands who blazed forward. They surrounded the mountain where the Archetype waited for the onslaught. As if knowing what was to come, Arc began to transfigure himself into a golden blazing warrior. Although similar to the others, his image was one of incredible beauty and strength. The change did not stop at the humanoid figure, but instead, he continued to morph until he was a glowing ball of nuclear fire. Zath and his thousands took formation as they surrounded Arc.

Without any warning, the battle began. It was unlike anything Oscar had ever seen. Like a wrecking ball of atomic fire, the Archetype used his blazing body to smash into those who had surrounded him. A tidal wave of light and sound pulsed outward. The explosion cracked and broke massive rocks loose from the mountain. It was barely possible to even understand the battle of blazing action that was taking place before Oscar's eyes.

The Archetype let out another powerful blast that knocked many of the golden warriors backward. Zath, at the center of the fray stood his ground. He deflected the fiery explosion by turning sideways and digging his heels into the rock.

"Compress!" Zath called to his soldiers over the noise. As soon as he did, the thousands of fighters tightened their circle around the Archetype. With each attack of Arc, the circle would grow tighter. He would blast, they would tighten. This went on for some time.

As the circle became more constricted, Zath and his six chief warriors produced a chain of fire. Oscar had not seen where it came from, nor had he ever seen anything like it. It was so dense that it took all seven of them to hoist. The other golden giants worked as a single unit to route and press the Archetype inward. Arc lashed out violently with fire and lightning against his captors, but the trap was beginning to crush his immeasurable power.

The roar of flaming battle scorched the rocks of the mountain where they neared it. Zath and his warriors squeezed in tighter as they constricted the orb of twisted light that the Archetype had made. When they were finally close enough, the thousands of golden warriors joined together by taking hold of one another to make a spherical net around the arc of evil. There was no way out for this ancient villain. The Archetype let out a mighty roar that sent ground quakes out in every direction. More rock broke and fell from the mountain.

Within a few seconds, the core of the heavenly force crushed in on the Archetype. Finally, they had sprung the trap. Although it didn't stop. Instead, tighter and tighter they squeezed. Once in place, more glowing soldiers poured onto the pile. They applied more pressure until the center began to approach a singularity. They crushed the Archetype back down.

When Arc was captured, Zath and his six golden men came forward with the fiery chain. Oscar reasoned that there must have been some extra-dimensional arrangement being exercised because he didn't fully understand what he was looking at. As best he could tell, Zath and his six soldiers wrapped the chain around the tightened circle that held Arc.

After another moment the scene was quiet. Oscar had not taken a single breath the entire time the battle had been happening. He waited for the signal, not sure if the battle was actually won.

After another instant he saw the double flash of light from General Zath. Oscar time-space jumped down to where they had the Archetype captured. His hands were trembling and his heart was beating rapidly. There was an electricity in the air. *What an honor to be here at such an occasion,* he thought.

There on the mountain, Zath's six warriors stood holding the flaming chain. At the center of the six-way web of fire was the archetype. Around his head was a fire muzzle. It was designed to keep him from misleading any others. Arc continued to struggle like a wild animal trapped in the brush. Oscar watched him, realizing it was almost impossible to find the words he had come to speak. The thousand other golden warriors stood ready overhead.

Like a million megaton flash, something happened. Oscar could not see. He tried to refocus his eyes on the scene in front of him, but the light was impossibly bright. He looked in the direction of Arc to see that no longer were Zath's warriors holding the chain of fire. Somehow, the Archetype had broken the hold. Zath and his six soldiers had been blasted back. The other golden warriors began to compress again, but the Archetype wasted no time. He let out a fiery blast from his body that sent many of them flying away.

Somehow, Arc broke loose of the fire muzzle and the chain completely. Oscar tried to take cover as the army of warriors pressed in tighter. He was in the wrong place at the wrong time. He could feel the time-space pressure of the golden army trying to press in on the place where he stood.

With another eruption of impossible heat, the Archetype exploded again, letting off more light and power than Oscar had ever seen at one time. The army that surrounded him faltered. It was all happening so fast that Oscar had no time to jump to safety. He felt the blast of white hot strength tear through his body. As he did, he let out a cry of distress.

Although Oscar could not tell what it was, in an instant, something changed. Like a molten meteor from the sky, a bolt of lightning and thunder zinged downward to the mountainside. The crunch of stone made the assembly of warriors stand still. Even the Archetype stopped to see who had arrived.

As the dust settled, Oscar could see two figures of great stature standing. Oscar had never met them personally, but he knew their names.

Makeal.

Gibreal.

They were the two high captains of the star-born armies, two among the most ancient twelve. The Archetype turned to face them both. They stood quietly regarding him. A knot twisted in Oscar's stomach at the sight of these three blazing warriors.

"Oh. My two little brothers have come," Arc said, now allowing his form to reshape. There was a family re-semblance between the three majestic creatures. Makeal and Gibreal stood as unimaginable statues of power and strength. They were the untarnished ones, who had stood in the greatest places of glory and fire and lived. They were the two burning suns. They had seen things that no other celestial but the Archetype had. The air was so alive with energy around them that it could have caught fire.

Makeal and Gibreal stood their ground as Arc stepped forward. "I could have made you gods of the Earth. I hope you got what you wanted for betraying me."

"The King rebukes you," Gibreal said as if Arc's words did not affect him. His voice came like the rushing of a powerful storm. The Archetype stepped closer still.

"You could have been worshipped as Poseidon and Hades, but you chose to forsake me, your own brother. We could have had it all," the Archetype said, but then added, "I'll offer you the same here. This world could be ours."

There was a long silence. It was Makeal that spoke this time. His booming voice echoed off the rock and rumbled down the mountainside. "The King rebukes you!" His shout could have melted pure stone and brought the stars to the surface of the world. Thunder rumbled as lightning arced across the sky.

Arc began to glow brighter now. He spat his words at the two heavenly brothers. "You and this entire army are not powerful enough to take me. I am the greatest-"

The action that followed cut his words off. Makeal shot forward. He moved so fast that his entire body was a blur. As he rocketed toward Arc, Gibreal burst into a white hot nuclear flame. Makeal began to orbit around Arc, moving faster and faster with every second. Gibreal wrapped himself around the Archetype, making a sphere as he attacked.

As Makeal gained orbital speed and Gibreal pressed in on Arc, the glowing point of light condensed down so small that those watching could no longer see anything but the impossibly bright dot of light. They pressed downward until the light was so hot that Oscar turned away to cover his face. He thought that the intense heat would melt the world. Waves of gravity and arcs of electricity shot from the point of light. Oscar was afraid that it would tear the world apart if it wasn't stopped.

With one final blast of light, Makeal and Gibreal were standing there again. They had done what the entire army could not. Each held out their hands, forming a dome around the glowing point of light. Arc was captured in a singularity. Oscar could understand why the ancients found it difficult not to worship these golden giants.

He stood struck dumb as he looked at the two powerful warriors. Zath came and paused next to Oscar. "You may now give the proclamation," Zath said. It took him a long moment to regain his composure. After gathering his wits, Oscar gave the address he had come for.

"Archetype of Evil, as regent of Newearth, I hereby banish you from the Kingdom, along with all cosmic time-space. First Prince Abriel, his Princess, and all of their siblings and descendants are under the protection of the High King himself. You will be removed in order that you may never tempt with twisted light again. Your captivity will be reinstated in the world of fire."

As soon as he finished his words, Makeal, Gibreal, Zath, and all of the other golden warriors were gone. Oscar stood alone on the mountain. He breathed a sigh of relief. "Thank you, my King," He said aloud. "The world is now truly ready for its first Prince."

INFINITE
TOMORROW

"Rise."

This time Abriel and Dawn were standing in a new place. The crowd, the brilliant light, and the Holy City itself was gone. They stood in a green glade with the King. They looked around surprised by the sudden change of scenery. Before they had time to take it all in, the King was speaking to them.

"I will give this land as the Nation of Abriel. You will rule it with wisdom and honor." He reached out and touched them both on the cheek. "I am with you always."

Abriel and Dawn knelt. They wanted nothing more than to please him.

"Rise," He said, a friendly chuckle in his voice. "I am your King, but I am also your friend."

"We want to be your friends forever," Abriel said. It sounded silly, but being in the presence of the king made him feel like a child.

"You have been loyal to me, and have obeyed my word. You will be my friends forever." He hugged them both. He then said, "Come, I will show you the Land of Abriel."

They smiled at each other, hardly able to believe the astonishing things that were taking place. It felt like a dream that could never end. With Myark, Estra, Thunder, and a host of Newearth's creatures, the King showed Abriel and Dawn the great land he had prepared for them.

CHRONICLES

THE KING BECAME THEIR teacher and taught them a great deal that they might build a nation that would walk by his glorious light. Abriel's garden brothers and Dawn's garden sisters became the princes and princesses of the twelve nations of Newearth. The King appointed Oscar as the ambassador of Newearth.

Abriel and his bride Dawn led the nation for twelve centuries.

They ruled with wisdom and honor, often bringing their splendor and grace to the Holy City.

Never was there a time when their faithfulness and loyalty were not being celebrated somewhere in the Kingdom.

Each of the princes of Newearth oversaw the cultivation of the world until it was completely gardened.

Each of the princesses of Newearth gave birth to many children who grew into the twelve nations of Newearth.

Abriel and Dawn worshiped and honored the King for all of the days of their mortal lives, until they were called to come live in the Holy City of the High King.

There will never be an end to the realm of the King. Forever, Amen.

A NOTE FROM THE AUTHOR

IT'S WORTH MENTIONING THAT this book is not eschatology, as some might assume. Eschatology is the Biblical study of the end times and what will come after. This book is instead a playground for experimenting with speculation about eschatological ideas. To aficionados of biblical end-times concepts who may feel tempted to dismantle this story with a fine-tooth comb, I'd say, "It's fiction, dude." It's not meant to teach exactly what will happen after Christ returns; it is meant to inspire believers to imagine how mysterious and glorious our future beyond His return may be. With that said, I'll show you a few examples where this book's speculation strays the farthest, while still within the realm of possibility.

I have invented several plot devices simply for the sake of the story, some that are fairly unlikely to take place in our actual future. Satan being brought back from the lake of fire to tempt future worlds, for instance, has a kind of template in Revelation's millennial kingdom, but does not seem likely after God creates the new heaven and new earth. However, for the sake of the narrative and to teach specific concepts about temptation and damnation, I opted to take a little creative license in that area of the story.

As you may have picked up from the book, in this fictional universe, there are humanoid beings other than those born on Earth. The Bible acknowledges the existence of angels, and we don't know where they were born, or even if they were. For this and other stories that take place in the same universe, I've invented the concept of Star-born and planet-born beings who serve God across many planets. Is this idea biblical? I like to think that ideas that the Bible is silent on, and do not violate biblical morality, are biblically permissible for fiction writers, even if the content would not be delivered from the pulpit.

The concept that the twenty-four elders will birth the children of the New Earth is pretty unlikely from a Biblical standpoint. The truth is, we don't know where the inhabitants of the New Earth will come from. God may create them anew, or they may be some remnant from this world, or some other option altogether.

These and a few other plot points are very speculative, but I think each falls within the realm of at least remote possibility when considering the known parameters of the Kingdom of God as it is described in the Bible. Now, I'd like to talk about what I hope this book will accomplish and why I think it would be an excellent gift for you to give to others.

The standard view of "heaven" in popular culture is that all the goodie-two-shoes will go and sit on clouds, play harps, and do nothing for eternity. This idea always bothered me and made me feel a little sick. After years of studying the Bible and the Kingdom of God, I concluded that those descriptions of Heaven were false and damaging to the Christian faith.

Undoubtedly, the future Kingdom of God will be much more than we can imagine. This book is designed to inspire and excite its readers about what possibilities might await us in the Kingdom of God.

If you are unfamiliar with the Kingdom of God, you should know a few things.

Jesus made it clear that to enter the Kingdom of God, that is, to have eternal life, all you must do is believe in Him. In the book of John, he says, "God loved the world so much that He gave his only son, that whoever believes in Him will not perish but have eternal life." So if you want to enter the Kingdom, you must believe in Jesus to receive eternal life.

All who believe in Jesus will have eternal life, but each person's experience will be different in the Kingdom. Jesus clarified that those who obey His word and are faithful to him in their mortal lives will be rewarded in the future Kingdom. Those who are faithful are described as good servants, joint heirs, rulers, and many other titles in the New Testament.

Believe in Jesus to receive eternal life. You are eternally secure once you've done that, but the story is just beginning. For those who have already believed, there is a universe of possibilities ahead. If you want to be rewarded and trusted with great responsibility in the Kingdom to come, then you must also follow him with your life.

I hope this book has inspired you to believe in Jesus (if you haven't yet) and encouraged you to live obediently in light of the glorious King Jesus and His Kingdom. I hope to see you in the Kingdom of God and can't wait to see what mysteries await us.

If you liked this book, please leave a review on the platform where you get your books. If you are interested in looking into one of the other many books I've written, please visit me at:

LUCASKITCHEN.COM

I look forward to seeing you again in the pages of a grand adventure. - Lucas Kitchen

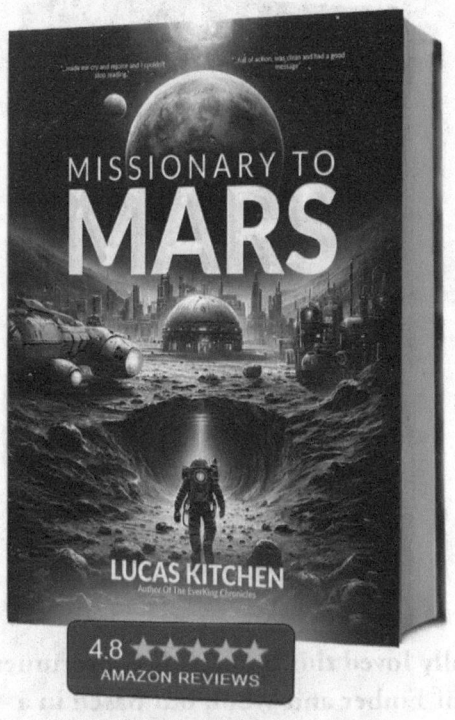

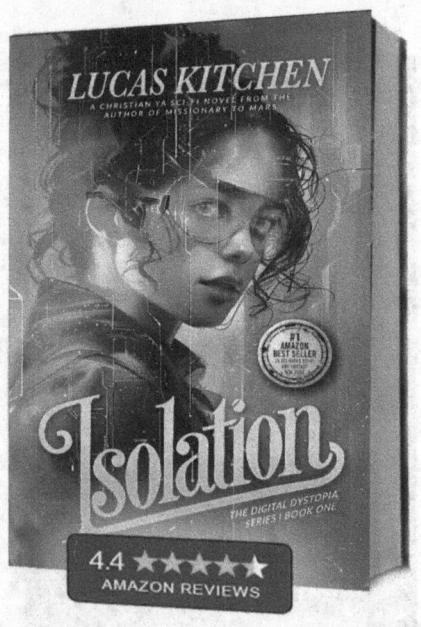

ABOUT THE AUTHOR

LUCAS KITCHEN IS AN American author of both Christian fiction and nonfiction. He has written over twenty books, and had some on Amazon's category best-seller lists. He writes blogs, releases podcasts, and publishes social media videos about Jesus, the faith, and Ai robots. His social media content occasionally goes viral. He lives in Texas with his wife, and four kids. You can see his books at Lucaskitchen.com.

www.ingramcontent.com/pod-product-compliance
Lightning Source LLC
Chambersburg PA
CBHW011453170626
46814CB00009B/3030